The Boys Book of Western Stories

Short Stories of the Old West

Edited by Frank Theodat & Zack Grafman

P3 Media Group LLC

Book Cover by Getcovers.com

Illustrations by Amanda Comntei

Contents

Acknowledgements

This anthology — this series, really—would not be possible without the support of an incredible team of people.

To my wife and son, for their love and support.

My sincere thanks to Sarah Grafman for proofreading this manuscript over the busy Christmas season. Your speed and thoroughness are nothing short of amazing.

To my Pulpeteer Brothers: Brady, Zack, James, and Frank, for their ongoing support, encouragement, faith and friendship.

All glory to God. May *The Boys Book Series* serve in accordance with His will.

The House That Pulp Built

INTRODUCTION

Included in this anthology are eight short stories: some new, some classic all set in the Old American West.

The Boys Book Series was created in hopes to inspire a love of reading in the next generation of young men through a classic genre of American literature: **Pulp Fiction.** *Adventure, Sea Stories, Western Magazine, Weird Tales,* and other publications dominated the publishing landscape from the 1920s and lasted for decades, in spinner racks, bus stations, drug stores, and newsstands. The pulp craze came to an end in the 1970s, but the legacy of pulp fiction cannot be ignored. Writer Harlan Ellison referred to comic books as America's literature, and the same can be said for the pulps.

Though the golden age has passed, pockets of pulp fans around the world continue to keep the tradition alive – both online and in person.

The Boys Book Series is our contribution preserving this nearly lost tradition.

Frank Theodat & Zack Grafman,

Editors, *The Boys Book Series*

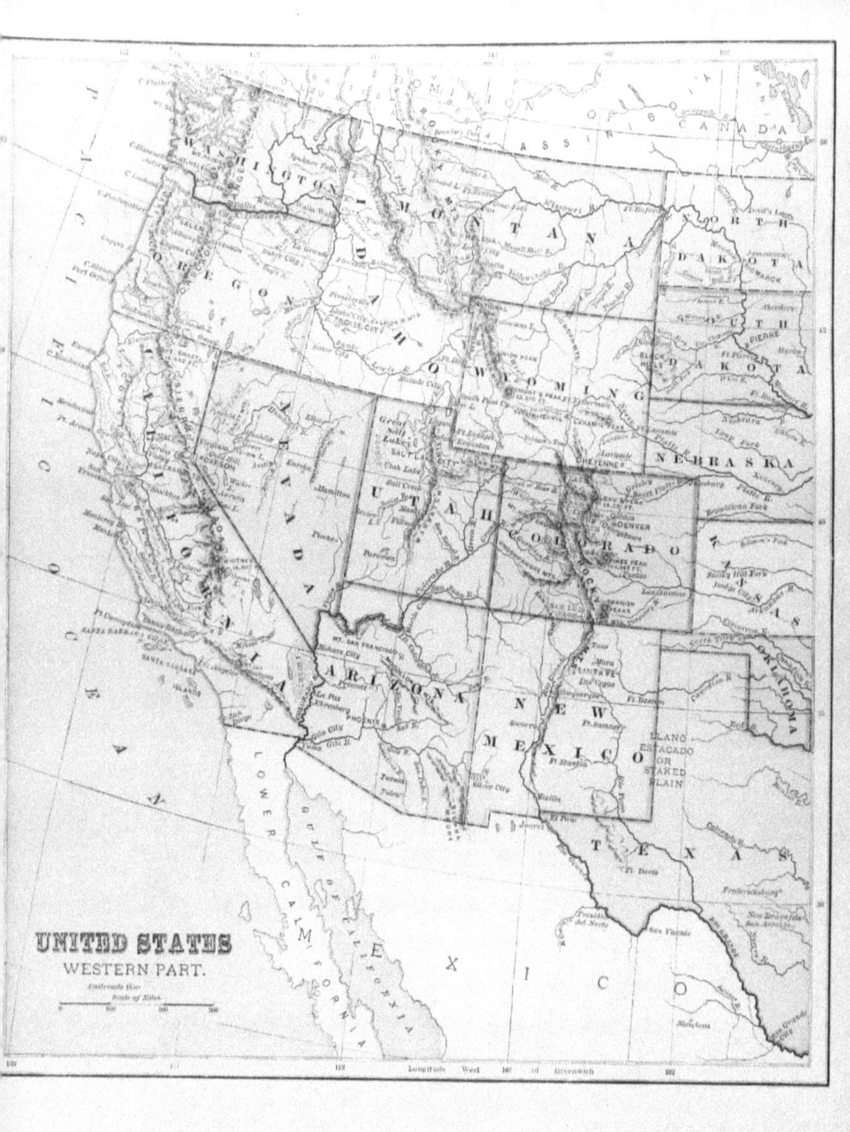
UNITED STATES
WESTERN PART.
WASHINGTON
OREGON
CALIFORNIA
NEVADA
IDAHO
MONTANA
WYOMING
UTAH
COLORADO
ARIZONA
NEW MEXICO
NORTH DAKOTA
SOUTH DAKOTA
NEBRASKA
KANSAS
OKLAHOMA
TEXAS
MEXICO
LOWER CALIFORNIA
GULF OF CALIFORNIA
PACIFIC OCEAN
ASSINIBOIA
CANADA
LLANO ESTACADO OR STAKED PLAIN
SALT LAKE CITY
DENVER
CHEYENNE
PHOENIX
BOISE CITY
SANTA BARBARA
Longitude West of Greenwich

To Kill a Banshee

FRANK KIDD

Sam flicked the end of his fishing pole as his fly touched the water. Little ripples arced outwards, reflecting the pinks and oranges of sunset. Sam leaned backwards and waited. The trout, having just begun to break water, would start feeding now that the sun had hurried its descent towards the horizon.

Someways away, just the other side of the narrow lake, a herd of wild mustangs came to water. The horses were a thing of beauty, selected by blizzard and heat and wolf and cougar, such that only the hardiest might survive. Yearling colts frolicked the bank, stamping in the far waters. Then they spooked, heads darting up, and just like that, they were gone, disappearing into the cottonwoods the way they'd come.

Next to him, ol' Rebel lolled lazily, his short blue-gray coat muddy from a day of traipsing the lake's bank. He panted, his sides vibrating from the evening's heat. The dog was pushing ten years, but he'd not lost a step, having retained almost all of his vital energy. In fact, the dog still looked just as fine as he ever had, his firm, tense muscles rippling beneath a beautiful blue-gray hide.

Rebel was a Blue Lacy, one of the descendants of the famed Lacy brother's hog dogs. Blue Lacys, like Sam himself, were borne of Texas, a mix of scent hounds, greyhounds, and quite possibly a coyote or two. They were bred for two things—herding cattle and hunting game. Lions, hogs, deer, raccoons... you name it, and a Blue Lacy could track it, chase it, or tree it.

The only sign Rebel was growing older was his new habit of napping on the porch swing and refusing to move over for Sam. Several times the old dog had grumbled at him for trying to move him. Sam had begrudgingly let him win these arguments, figuring the dog had earned the right to be a bit grumbly.

Sam, himself, was now pushing 16, which meant that he could not remember a day he'd not had the old dog by his side.

There was a quick tug on his line and Sam jerked the pole back, hoping to set the hook... he waited a beat... then came another quick couple of tugs... then the familiar thrashing that signaled a fish on the other end.

He had it!

A huge grin swept across his face as he pulled in the fishing line. Rebel was on his feet now as well, standing at the ready, unsure how he could help but nonetheless eager.

Sam banked the fish, careful-like, so that he wouldn't fall off and get away. It was a big one, nearly as long as two of his feet. He dug the hook from its throat with a pair of needle-nosed-pliers and then added him to the stringer.

It was nearly dark by this time, for the sun had fell fast, and the shadows of the mesas cast long and eerie over the West Texas plains.

"Let's get out of here," Sam said.

Rebel, the old soldier, rose and stretched his legs, then yawned.

At his horse, a paint pony he'd named Comanche, Sam slung himself up into the saddle. In the boot was his rifle, an old Henry Rifle. He patted the rifle's wooden stock as he turned Comanche onto the trail. Sam didn't like being out after dark unless he had to be, but if he did have to be, the rifle gave him an awful lot of confidence.

Sam's mind turned to his Pa then, the rifle being a gift from him. He'd gone off to drive cattle last spring. Now it was almost fall. He should've been back already... two months ago to be exact, but they'd still not got word of him. Ma had avoided the subject, and he could tell she was worried.

They were halfway home when the sun set fully, and with the darkness came a chill, and with the chill an even more uncanny feeling—one of being watched. It was as if the darkness watched them, or rather, something in the darkness. It was moving out there. A presence.

Sam heard Rebel growl. He felt it too, then, Sam thought, fear surging through his veins. He felt his hands go slick and clammy and he touched the Henry for a small hit of courage.

Then, from the darkness, came a blood curdling scream. A sound that could only come from a nightmare, as if a banshee or a cursed witch had been let loose from the very depths of hell.

Comanche bolted and Sam held on for dear life.

***

It was the fastest that Sam and Comanche had ever made it to the barn. Inside, Sam was so nervous that it took all of his focus to find the box of matches and get the lantern lit. When he did, the light only gave him some small part of his fear soaked sanity back.

Rebel stood at the door, looking outside, hackles raised, a low rumbling in his throat. He'd beat them back, somehow, no doubt taking a more straight-line to the barn than the one Comanche had. How he'd not fallen off he couldn't say.

"What the heck was that, boy?" Sam asked.

Again, as all the times before, Rebel just looked back at him, his eyes glossy, and caring, but uncommunicative. Well, that was perhaps not the proper description, for he often found that Rebel's eyes seemed to communicate so much, too much in fact, so that he could never quite decipher it all.

Sam took the rifle out of his saddle, cocked it, and set it aside. Then he went to work unsaddling Comanche and brushing him down. Every bone in his body wanted him to leave the horse for the morning. But he just couldn't do it, not to Comanche. The horse, like Rebel, was as much a part of him as anyone else. The three of them made a very merry band, like Robin Hood and Little John and the rest of his men.

He wondered if bullets could hurt things that went bump in the night. Banshees and spirits and such. Then he wondered if the scream had just simply been a woman? Maybe, one in trouble?

This thought brought him pause... but he brushed it off. For there were no neighbors anywhere near them. In fact, the closest thing to neighbors they had was the Reservation, and unless the Indians had jumped it again, they were not likely to be traipsing about.

Finally done with the horse, Sam grabbed the rifle and made for the house. Ma was inside, the cutting board ready for the fish. He handed them off, and she smiled. "Quite the catch today."

"Didn't get that big one until right before dark," Sam said.

"You go get cleaned up, and I'll get these started," she said.

Rebel, tuckered out from a long day of nothing, laid down on his bed in the corner—feed sacks stuffed with straw. One corner was ripped open where he had a habit of chewing at it. He never tore the whole thing up though, just worried at a corner, always the proper gent.

Sam ran water over his hands in the washbasin and listened to the clack of the knife as it came from the other room. He wondered if he should tell her about the scream.

Finally, he decided better of it. Pa had often said, "Son, no need worrying a woman about things you yourself can handle."

But could he handle whatever was out there?

***

Morning found him back atop Comanche, as they went to check the cattle grazing the far pastures. There'd been no more screams the night before, and Sam would know, for he'd only gotten a wink of sleep. Rebel was quite well-rested however, for he'd snored all night, as if totally unconcerned with the events of the night before.

It was about noon when he spotted the buzzards. They turned lazy circles up in the sky, riding the hot winds, circling something—something dead.

Sam grew increasingly uncomfortable as he approached. It was near the lake from the night before. The coincidence was too much, the blood curdling scream in the dark, the lake, and now... something was dead.

He guided Comanche down into the trees.

Above him, in the tree tops, the buzzards hopped from branch to branch, chittering away at each other like demons.

Comanche snorted and laid his ears back.

"Whoa, boy," Sam said, pulling the rifle from its boot. He cocked it, the sharp mechanical click making the buzzards take flight in a flurry of wings.

Comanche threw his head, snorting again. He was ready to spook.

"Alright, boy," Sam said, "you don't got to go no further. I won't make you."

Sam tied the horse off on a copse of juniper. Slowly, he plodded forward, deeper into the trees, the rifle held ready. He commanded Rebel to heel, and the old soldier obeyed, taking his place a few steps behind, hackles raised, nose searching the air.

Deep in the trees, right on the water's edge, he found a mess of blood in the leaves and a dark stain in the dirt. There'd been quite the scuffle, but no meaningful tracks.

Sam worked a circle around the bloody mess, analyzing it. He circled wider, and wider, finding no blood trail leading off in any other direction. He found no discernible tracks either, no sign of what had been killed or what had done the killing. Regardless, the earth was carved up something bad.

He was just about to give up, when he felt it—

A faint tap, a pitter-patter, on the brim of his hat. Something had just dripped on him.

A chill ran up and down his spine.

He looked up.

There, above him, hung the mangled body of a yearling colt, a swollen tongue hanging out of its mouth, eyes bulging in death. It had been dragged up into the tree and stashed firmly in the Y of its branches. Its neck was ripped wide open.

Sam jumped back and gave a small croaking scream that embarrassed him.

What kind of man screamed, he chided himself. He gripped the Henry tighter, and fought to regain his courage.

Steeling himself against the gruesome sight, he peered upwards, wondering what in the world had killed a yearling colt and dragged it up into a tree? And what had screamed like a banshee? What left no tracks like a ghost?

He didn't know, but he knew who might.

***

Sam rode onto the reservation driving three cows ahead of him just as his father often had. His pa was friendly with the Indians, and knew many of them from the old days before the Army and the reservation, when the buffalo still roamed the plains by the millions, and cattle, or "white horns" as the Indians called them, were only a dream.

Several women and children gathered around; they smiled and pointed at the gift of cattle that Sam drove before him. Some nodded at Sam, recognizing him from his many trips with Pa.

Rebel followed along behind, gathering pets from the children, his pink tongue hanging out of his head like he was the happiest gent in all of the west.

Calf's Heart lounged on the stoop of his clapboard house, a one bedroom sort of affair. He was once a powerful Kiowa War Chief, and now, a wise-man among the Indians.

Sam pulled rein in front of the old chief's lodge.

"Sam Erling?" Calf's Heart called. "Where have you been all summer. Where is your father?"

"Father's on a drive," Sam called, stepping off of Comanche.

"Come in, then," the old Chief bid.

Sam tied off Comanche and commanded Rebel to stay, and the old soldier obeyed, laying down just in front of Comanche.

Inside, Calf's Heart offered Sam the medicine pipe.

Sam hesitated, not sure if he should. His father had always smoked with the old Chief, and Sam had watched. Now he was here and—

"It is considered an insult to decline," Calf's Heart said, registering Sam's hesitation.

"Oh, no offense meant," Sam said, "I guess I... never mind." He took the pipe. Puffed. And then coughed as the old Chief laughed.

"Your father should be back already, no?" Calf's Heart asked.

"Well, yeah. A month ago," Sam said.

The Chief nodded, his eyes registering the implications. "And you, you're running the whole place then?"

"It's easy enough for the most part, Pa took most of the cattle with him."

"This is good," the Chief said. "You are a man now, no?"

"I don't feel like a man," Sam said.

The Chief chuckled. "Then what has brought you, Sam Erling, to visit the Kiowas?"

Sam took another puff and managed not to cough this time, then he launched into his story. He told the old Indian about the scream, and the dead colt, and that there were no tracks, and how it was most certainly—

"It's a lion," the Chief said, cutting his speculation short.

"You mean a catamount?" Sam said, the whole affair becoming somewhat obvious to him in hindsight. "But that terrible scream?"

"That's the noise a lion makes," Calf's Heart replied somberly. "But it's not any lion."

"What do you mean?"

"A month ago it killed Red Flower. Then, a week ago, two children went missing by the river. We found only blood. But we also found tracks." Calf's Heart held up his hand and spread his fingers wide, "Huge paws, as big around as my hand."

"So it's a man-eater?" Sam asked, breathless.

Calf's Heart nodded solemnly. "You and your mother are not safe up there. Once a man-eater gets a taste for human flesh, there is nothing to stop it. Nothing but a bullet."

"But the colt?" Sam asked.

"Half-eaten?" Calf's Heart asked.

Sam nodded.

"Just enough to satisfy its hunger. It was hunting you last night. It will be back."

Sam stood suddenly. "I got to warn Mother."

"Wait," the Old Chief said, raising a hand. "Before you go." He shuffled towards a leather parfleche in the corner of the room. Out of it, he pulled a leather thong strung with the fangs and claws of a mountain lion. "This is strong medicine. I traded twenty horses to Quanah Parker, the great blue-eyed war chief of the Comanches, for it. It is said, that the one who wears the totem in battle will not be wounded. That he will have the protection of the lion. Bring it back to me when you've killed the beast."

Sam took the necklace from the old man and slipped it over his head. He felt the power in it, or at least imagined he did. Then, just as he was about to turn, the old Indian caught up his arm and pulled him close. He whispered something into Sam's ear, only for him to hear.

The boy's eyes went wide, and then he nodded at the Indian.

Outside, he mounted Comanche and whipped the horse to a thundering gallop.

***

He found his mother outside, sitting in the porch swing, a shotgun laid across her lap.

"Ma!" he called, jumping off the back of Comanche.

"Where you been?" she called, standing. Her hair was a mess and she looked flustered.

"Ma, you need to be inside, there's a man-eater about."

"A what?"

"A mountain lion," Sam said, breathless. "I should have told you last night, but—"

"I just shot at it."

"You what?"

"The lion," his ma said, lifting the shotgun. She pointed off towards the west. "It came after me when I was hauling water, but I was damn near inside the house when it made its move. I slammed the door on it, grabbed the gun, and shot at it."

Sam stood mouth agape for a second, having never heard her swear before, then asked, "Well did you hit it?"

"I don't know. I don't think so. It took off though."

"Me and Rebel are going after it."

"You'll do no such thing, young man," his mother chided.

Sam turned, and looked at her, his eyes narrowing, "I got to. And I need you to go inside while I go to it. Pa ain't coming back. I know it. You know it. And even if he is, we can't wait around for him no more. I'm here, and it's up to me."

She started to say more, but Sam was already back atop Comanche, already whirling the horse in the direction she'd pointed. He was already a man.

***

It was called the Ciudad de las Montañas by the Indians, which translated to City of the Mountains. Legend had it that the Spanish first discovered it, and by then it was already ancient. And it was not really a mountain of course, for Texas was sparse on mountains, but it was high up in a rock canyon, on the edge of a mesa. Old Indian ruins built into the high sides of the mesas. Ruins that were older than the

Comanche, the Kiowa, and the Spanish combined. It was three days of trailing the big cat before they came to the place.

Sam brushed the dust away from his clothes as he looked up at the ancient Indian city. The black windows in the stone forts stared back down at him like so many shiny eyes.

His stomach growled. The last thing he'd eaten was a tough old jackrabbit early yesterday. He'd split it with Rebel, but there wasn't much to split since the big Henry had dang near disappeared the front half of it.

Rebel looked up at him, his tongue hanging out, and he seemed to be smiling, looking as if he was just having the time of his life. The old soldier loved to work. He lived and breathed the hunt, and once he'd caught the old cougar's scent, he'd not let go of the trail.

Every so often Sam would find a paw print or a tuft of fur, and confirm that Rebel was still onto the ghost. And now, almost thirty miles and three days later, the mountain lion seemed to be slowing.

They moved on up the winding trail and towards the ruins. Rebel sniffed the ground ahead of them. Several times he lost the scent, but every time he'd work larger and larger circles all over the hillside until he found it again.

Sam would wait for him, sitting silently atop Comanche, his rifle across his lap, his face set towards the top.

Finally the trail narrowed until they were riding along the cliff face of the mesa. There was nowhere for man, horse, dog, or mountain lion to have taken anything but the trail. It made sense why stone age man had built his fortress up here. There was only one way up, and it was an easy enough place for only a few men to defend.

Soon enough, the trail widened, and they rode straight through the mud and rock ruins of the ancient fortress. Mud and stone parapets. Windows. Old stone cooking circles. It was a haunted sort of place.

In several places, he found the broken remains of wooden stockades where animals of one sort or another had once been kept.

The ruined shelters were squat affairs, roofless, no doubt once covered with thatch. Their floors dusty. Stone benches carved into the rock wall of the mesa.

It was an exceedingly strange place. Both crude and advanced all at once. He could almost feel the soul of the place, surely haunted with ghosts of an ancient race long past.

A little further up, he passed the last of the ruins and the trail once more narrowed to just a horse width. The rock wall was covered with old aboriginal paintings. Swirls of paint and flowers. Men hunting buffalo and elephant like creatures. Mammoths perhaps? He'd heard of the wooly beasts in his science reader.

A little further on and he saw the very top of the mesa, and there, beneath a jagged, tumble of boulders sat the black maw of a cave.

Rebel whined, and kicked out his back feet as if readying to charge upwards.

"Hold steady, boy," Sam said. He glanced around then, noted the setting sun. Perhaps an hour or two of day light left. Hardly enough to risk tangling with the man-eater in the dark.

That night, both he and Rebel sat by the fire. They gathered bits of wood from an old stockade and built a big, bright orange fire in one of the stone pits. The fire made him feel better. Comanche stood guard nearby, his ears flicking back and forth. His nose buried in the feed sack draped over his head, contentedly eating a few handfuls of corn.

Sam carefully cut the sleeves from his shirt and then cut the cloth down further into long strips. These he dipped the in the whale oil that he always carried for the purpose of cleaning his rifle. When the cloth strips were nice and oily he gently wrapped them around the end of four sticks, making his own torches.

He then set them aside and admired his handiwork. Rebel crawled closer to him, laying his head in his lap. Sam moved the rifle, making room for the old soldier.

"You better be careful tomorrow," he said. "We've been through too much together."

Rebel looked up at him, and then yawned, his eyes drooping sleepily.

Suddenly, Sam felt an impulse to call it off. They'd chased the old cat this far. Surely he'd stay away. How could he ask Rebel to go up there with him and face down such a beast, a man-eater to boot.

Perhaps, tomorrow they would call it off and ride away. Then he remembered his mother's worried face. The fact it had stalked him... stalked her. He thought of the Indians it had dragged away. And he wondered if he could do such a thing. If he could turn and go from what was demanded. His words come back to haunt him: "I got to."

"When a man says something, he does it," his Pa had always said.

Suddenly, an idea. Sam took Calf's Heart's medicine off from around his neck, and tied it around Rebel's. "There you go boy, better you than me. Ol' Henry here can be my medicine." He patted the rifle.

Rebel merely readjusted his head, appearing none the wiser at his new powers.

Sam looked around then, at the old ghostly ruins. It would normally be a hard place to sleep, the ruins of a long ago place with a man-eater stalking the dark.

But they'd been on the trail for three days. They'd ate twice, and were bone tired, and on some level Sam didn't care what happened tonight as long as he could get some sleep. The ghosts could wait and so could the cougar. There was a lesson in that. Something about being too tired to be scared, he thought. That, or courage came easy to the well-worked. Either way, Sam felt sleep claiming him.

***

It seemed like he'd just shut his eyes when he heard the worried whinny of Comanche and heard the quick a rush of movement.

His eyes went wide, and the first thing he noticed was how low the fire had burned down. *How long had he slept?*

Faintly, he saw Comanche whirl on his lead and kick out at something. Then he heard a purring growl come from the outer dark as the big cat circled around.

Rebel was on his feet, hackles raised, a low growl in his throat.

Sam snapped up the rifle and fired it off towards the cat.

Then he saw it, a tawny shadow disappearing in the inky blackness.

Rebel took off after it and Sam called out for the old soldier to wait, but he knew it was no use. The dog had the cat's scent, and he'd seen him. Now it was time to kill and the old boy would neither stop nor listen to a command until he caught that cat.

Sam plunged a torch into the glowing coals and then sprinted up the trail, the Henry in one hand, Rebel's deep solemn bark someway up ahead.

It was a hard climb through the rock field, made even harder in the dark. Several times he busted a knee, or a shin, or twisted an ankle as he climbed up the tangled mess. His knuckles bled from where he scuffed them on the boulders. To all of this he paid little attention; instead he focused on the steady braying of Rebel and prayed that it wouldn't stop. The dog had the old cat cornered. That's what that braying meant. It also meant that ol' Rebel was in trouble if he tried to push the cat too hard.

Sam found Rebel standing at the mouth of the cave barking into the black maw. At it's mouth, the torchlight almost refused to penetrate the darkness.

Sam cocked the rifle and slid forward, holding the rifle steady in the crook of his left arm, his left hand holding the torch forward. It was an awkward position, but workable.

Somewhere inside the darkness came a snarl and a hiss. Sam gulped, and Rebel barked even harder, his back legs scratching the dirt like a bull readying to charge. Then, without any more warning, Rebel launched forward into the cave and Sam swore.

Sam charged forward, the torchlight whipping in front of him and almost going out. The cave's walls were covered in old Indian paintings and the floor crunched underfoot. Sam glanced down, drawn by the noise—ivory bones, thousands of them. His feet sent one clattering across the others. He swallowed hard, and continued on.

Then, rounding a bend in the cave, he found Rebel barking into the darkness.

Sam waved the torch back and forth but the fire light could not illuminate far enough back into the cavern to see anything.

Rebel was barking upwards.

It must be a stone ledge. On this hunch, and before he could think it through, Sam threw the torch upwards.

There was a snarl as the flaming brand almost hit the big cat. It landed someways behind the beast on whatever stone ledge it occupied.

Sam could now see the cat pace back and forth, back lit as it was by the dying torch. Big heavy shoulders churned like pistons and from tip to tail it looked to be almost eight feet long.

Rebel barked and brayed, and Sam shouldered the Henry, aiming more by feel then by sight for it was too dark to use the irons... he fired.

Thwap.

He cocked the rifle and chambered another round as the cat came snarling forward off the ledge.

Sam was sure it would get to him, but Rebel met it half way, all one hundred pounds of him slamming hard into the tawny missile.

Both dog and cat rolled, and Sam leveled the rifle again, but he didn't dare fire lest he accidentally hit Rebel.

The whirling mass of cat and dog went round and round, with a hiss, snarl, and a bark, until Sam couldn't take it any longer. He dove forward, jamming the rifle barrel down hard into the back of the whirling cat.

The cat scrambled backwards, before turning to face him.

In the dim light, Sam saw a huge fanged mouth open and hiss.

Then it lunged. A paw he'd not seen swiped him hard and he felt pain flare across his chest. He fell backwards, firing as he did so, point blank into the big cat.

Then Rebel was back into the mix. He slammed hard into the big cat before it could finish its lunge, but it was already over. The big cat fell over lifeless, Sam's final shot having done its worst.

Rebel stood haughtily over the dead beast, triumphant.

Fetching the torch, Sam held it near the big cat's body. His first shot had hit him towards the back, a gut shot that did very little but piss the thing off. His second shot had been pointblank and had no doubt hit the heart. He could tell by the deep red blood pooling beneath the cat.

Slowly, Sam examined the rest of the cave. Then he found a doll—an Indian girl's doll—and some old shreds of buckskin clothing.

***

Sam and Rebel sat by the fire. This had been the final command of the old Indian, the one he'd whispered to him. "Cook the lion's heart. It will give you great power. Very strong medicine. To not do this is to be haunted by its spirit."

Sam cut off a piece and tasted it. It tasted good, a rich and chewy meat. Tougher than he expected. He cut a piece off for Rebel too. The dog snapped it down and then stood at attention.

Somehow, and Sam would never be able to explain it, Rebel did not have a single scratch on him. Where the cat had opened his own chest up with a single swipe, Rebel had gone toe to toe with the thing and not suffered so much as a nicked ear.

Sam untied the Kiowa totem and removed it from Rebel's neck. Then Rebel's ears perked, and he lifted a nose to the night, nostrils flared and searching the air.

Then from the darkness come a familiar voice, "Ahoy the fire."

Sam stood quickly, the blood rushing to his head. "Pa, is that you?"

A figure stepped into the firelight and smiled. "Looks like I showed up a tad late to help."

"Pa!" Sam exclaimed. "You're alive."

"Your mother sent me after you," Pa said.

"She mad?" Sam asked.

"Just worried," Pa said.

The End

The Weight of a Star

BLAKE BOBECHKO

The frontier was the shoreline of a windswept and flowered sea of grass, dotted by islands of poplar groves as far as the eye could see. Buffalo wallows and tea-stained creeks were her deepest basins. You could see a storm brewing from leagues away; sometimes a few at a time, hoping to meet up like friendly mutuals and blur the division between earth and sky. There were only a handful of white settlements on the plains back then. Young men were made to be farmers and lawmen, both at the same time if they wanted to reach manhood.

That rustling sea was where young William Brown had hailed from. Bill's family had been homesteaders in what was then called Montana Territory. Bill was the name his pa and his sister Alice affectionately called him. Bill's ma had gone to be with the good Lord when he was just six years old; when Alice was just three. Rocky Mountain Spotted Fever the neighbours called it, to be sure. "Nothing nobody could do," Pa would say regretfully at the funeral. He had been praying for a miracle.

Despite their good distance from what some folk call *civility*, the farm was never completely isolated from people's comings and goings. There was always work to be done, and Pa always had a few farmhands whom he'd hire for a season or two. Usually passersby; rarely on word of mouth. Bill's pa would put them up in their own comfortable lodgings in the barn tack room.

That year, Bill's pa had hired a real colourful fella who went by the name of Dan Maramec, a half-breed Indian with a wandering eye – always made Alice feel uncomfortable. But since Dan was already the name of the man on the next farm over, a goodly man who wouldn't want his name tarnished, Bill's pa distinguished his hireling as *Confederate* Dan on account of him bragging to the kids that he had fought for the South and had never surrendered. When Bill first told his pa about Dan's past, his father had only nodded knowingly, saying that since God had forgiven him, he had an obligation to forgive others. But Bill and Alice knew that Dan was still as yellow-bellied as they come. The kids called him *Injun* Dan, because he was mighty proud of being of the Piikani nation too.

On the day after Bill's sixteenth birthday, he had left the homestead on his own for the first time. He had saddled up his steed Will (that was what Bill named his horse on account of nobody else using the good name) and had ridden out for the last leg of a cattle drive, which had started in Texas that spring and was only now nearing its destination. His pa had assured him that the farm would be in good hands until he returned for the harvest, as he had *Confederate* Dan around to assist with the workload. And faithful to his promise, Bill (and Will) had arrived back by early September while the crops were ripe in the fields.

You could see a rider coming from miles away on those open plains, and so Bill's spirit became troubled as he approached the quieted homestead without a welcoming reception. He would stubbornly brush aside those awful thoughts which can arise when you're worried about your kin. But this time he'd be justified in thinking the worst, for what he discovered would quickly turn Bill's world upside down.

Finishing his lonely approach, he saw that somebody was laying across the porch steps, eerily motionless. Bill spurred Will to hasten his pace.

At the house, Bill leapt from his saddle. But he was stopped cold, as he discovered that his dear pa had been murdered; gunned down in cold blood.

Bill's mind raced.

He hollered out for Alice. Then he scoured the property, checking the house first, then the barn stalls and finally, cautiously, the tack room. His sister was nowhere to be found. Neither were the farmhands. The homestead was completely abandoned. Could have been for days. Even pa's horse was missing.

Bill returned to his father's body to see what might be seen.

A spent percussion cap was left by his pa's stiffened body. It cried out to Bill like a tattletale. The shot was doubtless from Injun Dan's .36 brass framed Colt. Dan had bragged on more than one occasion about having gotten that six-shooter from his time with the Confederacy. That gun was the only one Bill had ever seen quite like it.

The best that Bill could reckon was that Injun Dan must have gotten into some dispute with Pa over his earnings and that it turned ugly. Alice was no doubt taken by the bandit for recompense.

This is what brought Bill to the United States Marshal's office in Coulson. And this was the series of events which led to Bill being deputized to accompany marshal Obadiah Goodnight deep into Blackfoot territory, a place where white settlers often feared to tread.

***

"Are you going to uphold the Constitution of these United States and her territories?" Obadiah gruffly demanded of young Bill, following this short account.

"What do you mean?" Bill asked, more than a little perplexed by the suddenness of the demand. The marshal's office smelled of pine and tobacco, a familiar combination. Bill's mind was recalled to his father labouring in the barn back home.

"Do you swear?" Obadiah insisted with a steely gaze, causing Bill to stammer backward. The marshal was a large, imposing and weathered-looking man, with crows' feet impressed upon lean boney face, his leathery cheeks covered by a grizzled beard. On his head he wore a dirty old Union cap. From his hip hung a big iron, with "Rom 13:4" carved into its wooden grip.

Bill paused for a moment, realizing that he was being deputized. "Yes, I suppose I do," he thought aloud.

"So help you God." Obadiah huffed as he reached into his pine desk drawer for a star, which he promptly pinned onto Bill's wool vest.

At the sight of that star, Bill's mind was immediately recalled to glorious tales of lawmen and outlaws, especially those stories of Texas which he had soaked up on those cool nights around the fire during the cattle drive that summer; stories which you, reader, might find in this very book!

Bill caressed the silvery star, measuring its weight in his hand.

"It's lighter than I thought one would be," he remarked, still a little surprised by the marshal's efficiency. "What do I need this for?" He finally asked.

"Killing ain't always murder, son. It's the difference between a hanging and a lynching. And we're not hosting no necktie social. If this Dan did it, then he'll face justice. You're a strong arm of the law now."

Bill looked at his star, pondering those words while Obadiah chewed the cud. He thought of his sister Alice and what might have become of her.

"There's already a bounty on this 'Injun' Dan's head," the marshal elaborated. "Goes by Daniel Atkins sometimes. He's already wanted for drunkenness, indecency, robbery, Lord knows what else. Now we'll add murder and kidnapping to the list. Disappeared for a while, apparently finding work on your daddy's farm. That's established now on the basis of two witnesses: you and your poor old daddy's body. Only I've never seen him, but you have."

Outside the marshal's office, Bill breathed deeply as he contemplated what might have come of his sister. Pa had brought him to the mercantile in Coulson a few times before. But this was his first time in Coulson alone. Bill looked around the town with fresh eyes. There wasn't a church or a school, like you might expect to find. Just a few fresh pine buildings and worker tents pitched along the Yellowstone River. But there were already plenty of saloons in operation. A good place for a lawman's business, Bill thought.

Bill introduced Obadiah to trusty Will, who had stood tethered to the porch rail during their meeting. He showed the marshal his father's levered Winchester, which had been saddled up to his faithful horse.

"It's enough." Obadiah approved with a nod.

***

The trail north of Coulson was dusty and not heavily trodden.

Obadiah sat atop a big chestnut-colored gelding named Busefalus, something to do with an ox-head branded on its thigh. Busefalus carried the marshal's large frame effortlessly. Bill had never seen a prouder horse or so noble a rider.

Will kept pace to the rear, bouncing his master in the saddle; Bill always keeping a finger or two loosely pressed on his Winchester's stock, ready to pull it from its scabbard at moment's notice.

Between the two riders, they had rationed a few weeks' supply of hardtack, buffalo jerky, and four canteens. One of Obadiah's saddlebags was dedicated solely to plugs of tobacco, and Bill had stowed away some crab apples as treats for the horses.

On that first day, the riders seldom paused, save for an opportune moment at a creek to let the horses drink and refill their canteens.

The marshal had said little since pinning the star on Bill, only that Blackfoot country was no place for loud mouths or slow hands. But that night, by firelight, Obadiah began to explain their situation.

"You mentioned that Dan was half Piikani," he asserted, not looking up.

Bill nodded, staring into the flames. "That's right," he finally replied, worn out from the hard day of riding.

"That's why we headed north." Obadiah explained. "He would have only gone one way if he's running from the law. But Dan knows this country better than us... and his kin might hide him. Going to be difficult prying him away, wherever he's holed up."

Obadiah spit a brown pool in the dirt.

"Best bet is to start looking for your sister. A white girl in Blackfoot Confederacy country will stand out like a sore thumb. Dead or alive, someone will have noticed her. That trail will lead us to him."

Bill's mind wandered. He thought about he and Alice playing in the barn loft when they were young. He thought about his pa, and about what might happen to the farm now that he was gone. Obadiah had quietly dispatched the town's undertaker to collect his father's body before they had left Coulson. Bill wondered what kind of state the undertaker would find Pa in. It all felt like a bad dream.

With little else spoken between them, Bill whispered a quiet prayer and was soon asleep.

The two of them rode a discouraging three days northbound, without the grace of a sign.

On the fourth day, a grizzled trapper named McPhee told them about a half-breed matching Dan's description who had traded a woman's calico dress for whiskey at a Métis camp near Musselshell.

Bill recalled that familiar sounding name from boyhood, when his family would gather around the hearth and Pa would tell stories about the plains. Musselshell had been aptly named by those great explorers Lewis and Clark for its freshwater mussels which lined its riverbank in quantities. Pa said that they were delicious.

They found the camp at dusk—teepees in a half-circle, cook-fires smoking, dogs barking at the strangers. A thickset Métis trader stepped forward, palm out. Obadiah spoke French, then a smattering of Blackfoot. Money changed hands. The trader pointed north and west, toward the Bears' Paw Mountains.

"Two days hard ride," Obadiah translated. "Dan's rendezvous'd with Crowfoot at one of their councils."

Bill became nervous. Chief Crowfoot had a reputation for being a shrewd diplomat on account of him being an even fiercer warrior.

"Should I hide my badge?" he asked.

"No!" Obadiah firmly corrected. "You mustn't do that. It's liable that the only thing keeping you alive out here is that star."

Bill looked confused.

"People tend to think twice about their actions when they know that they'll be looking over their shoulder till kingdom come." Brown spittle ran down Obadiah's grey-streaked beard as he pivoted the talk. "Trader says we can camp here tonight. I'd prefer setting up a little outside. Maybe down by the bend in the river."

Though the sun was setting, Bill's mind prioritized mussels. His mouth watered at the prospect of fresh, cold game after days of hot dusty travels, often with a parched throat.

While Obadiah set up camp, Bill went down to the riverbank. At the bend, he discovered a deep looking pool, well set back from the seam of the river. In the midst of that pool he spied an old rail post barely poking out from the water. That post had likely been discarded from the camp some time ago, but with only a little effort, Bill was able to dislodge it from the accreted bed. To his delight, the wood was covered in pearl shells, mussels just like his father had told him.

Bill produced a knife from his vest and began to pry open his wild game.

The mussels were tough; leathery enough that Bill fancied he must have looked like the marshal chewing the cud. But they were cold and immensely refreshing.

***

The Bears' Paws stood like lonely snowcapped islands on the plains; unlike any other range Bill had laid eyes on before. Indian legend said that their posterity was spared there, when the Great Spirit slew a bear to save their ancestor. Bill perceived a spiritual heaviness as they approached those Canaannite High Places, a feeling which grew every mile or so, and intensified as they ascended the Bears' Paw.

Like the landscape, the weather was also changing. Winter had begun to announce its soon arrival, with the dew of colder evenings lingering as frost late into the mornings.

Riding so steep an incline brought its own physical challenges, but no situation arose which Bill and Will failed to muster themselves. Though the pair couldn't have foreseen it that past summer, the cattle drive had proven itself providential in preparing the horse and his young rider for what laid ahead.

From a dry riverbed, the riders would finally approach the Blackfoot council's encampment – teepees in a half-circle, cook-fires smoking not completely dissimilar to that Métis camp, days earlier. But as they approached, Bill's countenance lifted. For even from afar, he immediately recognized Alice. Though she was dressed like a squaw, her yellow hair contrasted the blackened hair of all the other girls.

Alice was sitting on the ground, apparently bound because her hands were hidden from sight. She was positioned in front of the most prominent teepee amid the camp.

That must be where Dan is holed up, Bill thought to himself.

The marshal had spied the girl too. Without a shared word, he knew what the boy was thinking.

As the riders continued to near, they were intercepted by Blackfoot warriors, each of them clad in bison skins with soft hide moccasins. Barbarians they were, yet dignified in their appearance, each of them men of valour, impressing the image of the noble savage.

Bill and Obadiah were received without a word exchanged. The riders were made to dismount, and their horses were led with care into the midst of the camp where little Indian children were playing. Bill watched as his Winchester dangled in its scabbard, abandoning him to the mercy of his hosts. Little good it would serve him now.

As one of the savages reached for the big iron on Obadiah's hip, the marshal stared him down with the concentrated authority of the United States government. So steely was his gaze that the Blackfoot stammered backward. Recognizing the marshal's office, he refrained.

Pa's horse began to whinny and neigh at the sight of the boy.

Alice's eyes grew wild when she saw her brother approach, accompanied by a lawman. In shock, she didn't speak a word.

Bill put his finger to his hushed lips as he approached, hoping to reassure his sister, as he and Obadiah were led to that most prominent teepee, and the door flap was lifted for them to enter.

Inside, the lodgings were dark and rank smelling. Bill's eyes burned from the smoke.

Around a smouldering fire, on an earthen floor, sat perhaps a dozen more warriors, each of them apparently men of high regard, for at their centre, across from the door flap, sat Chief Crowfoot. Beside him cowered Injun Dan; or Confederate Dan; or Dan Maramec; or Dan Atkins. Have your pick. Bill pointed him out to the marshal.

Though the great Siksika chief remained cross-legged, his posture communicated tremendous strength, his placement among them established like a cottonwood on the plain, its roots widespread and its limbs heavy with the snow of many winters, yet unbowed by the fiercest winds of change. His gaze was full of sorrow and resolve, for only a true warrior is capable of being a peacemaker, and each of the men surrounding Crowfoot were like arrows in his quiver, ready to do his will.

Obadiah removed his dusty old union cap out of respect for his host. Yet he remained standing. Bill, who had been watching the marshal for cues, stood nervously beside him.

The chief began to speak in a low, powerful voice.

"I had been informed of your coming some days ago," Dan's voice cracked as he interpreted, seeing the Obadiah had maintained the big iron on his belt.

The marshal got straight to the point.

"We've come to take a prisoner to face justice," he replied, eyes locked on the chief while his finger pointed at the interpreter to ensure the message would be rightly delivered.

The chief's response was defiant, though Obadiah perceived that Dan lacked the courage to deliver the message with its full force. With ice in his veins, the marshal spoke back that he would not permit any backtalk, and that he would most certainly be leaving with Dan in custody.

Crowfoot shot to his feet to meet the marshal eye to eye. His warriors followed suit, all his men except the cowardly Dan who quietly shouldered his way to the background.

The marshal stood head and shoulders above the lot of them, undaunted by their numbers. Without breaking his gaze, he waved the chief backward, letting him know in no uncertain terms that if he or his men were to strike, then it would undoubtedly be Crowfoot who would suffer first. He waited for Dan to translate, then he ordered Bill to open the door flap, letting light enter uncomfortably.

As Bill held the flap, his knees knocked together from fright. But as he bravely stood his ground, the silver star he wore glinted in the light, its reflection dancing around the higher parts of the still darkened lodge.

Crowfoot counselled his men in words unintelligible to Bill.

Then the marshal pushed his way through the warriors with the confidence of God's own minister of justice and stepped up to his man.

"Well Dan, I see you've swapped one confederacy for another."

Injun Dan pulled his .36 brass framed Colt, intending to stuff its nose into the marshal's belly, point blank.

Almost mechanically, the marshal slapped the criminal's piece to the ground, not even reaching for his own.

"Yankee scum!" Dan muttered rebelliously, getting spit in Obadiah's eye.

Obadiah seized Dan by his collar, and dragged him out of the hostile lodge. No further objections were made by Crowfoot or his warriors.

Bill nervously stepped out of the teepee, ahead of the marshal and his prisoner, almost tripping over Alice who had been desperately listening by the door, praying to be liberated by her brother.

"Daniel Atkins," Obadiah spoke. "you're under arrest for murder, kidnapping and a whole bill of law-breaking which don't begin to sum up your treasonous hide."

"Hang me, then. Or shoot me. Makes no never-mind." Dan replied as he grinned hopelessly at Alice.

Bill unbound his sister from her leather cords as she wept from relief, hiding her face from the wretched man.

Before the crowd of quieted Blackfoot onlookers, which now included the women and children, Bill helped Alice onto Will's back.

Bill mounted his pa's horse, finding its saddle no longer too big for him.

Obadiah clamped cold irons onto Dan's wrists and threw him over the back of Busefalus.

***

Folks came from many miles to Coulson to see the hanging of Daniel Atkins — homesteaders, drovers, even the Métis trader. Dan begged the judge for mercy after receiving the forgiveness of both Bill and Alice. The judge said that mercy was the job of the clergy; that he bore the civil sword and had sworn an oath to wield it well.

Most of the onlookers to Dan's hanging attended a delayed funeral for Bill and Alice's father. The undertaker had kept their pa's body on ice. Bill and Alice buried Pa proper, beside their ma under a cottonwood on the farm.

In their absence, Bill and Alice's goodly neighbours (the untarnished Dan and his family) had harvested their late father's crop and, after the funeral, had placed the earnings from its sale directly into Bill's hands, clear of charge.

On the evening of the funeral, once most of the visitors had departed, Obadiah found Bill on the porch steps, staring over those great plains as the sun set. His mind churning on next years crop and counting his blessings.

"Too bad we'll never know what Crowfoot said to his men, to just let us go like that." Bill said aloud as Obadiah sat next to him.

"I've only got a skin-deep handle on Blackfoot speech, boy. But they were talking about our stars. How killing a star only brings more of them... People tend to think twice about their actions when they know that they'll always be looking over their shoulder till kingdom come." Obadiah spit some brown juice into the earth.

Bill marveled at what he said.

"Star still feel light?" the marshal finally asked.

Bill had been carrying the badge in his pocket ever since the hanging. He pulled it out and turned it over in his fingers. "Feels like it weighs the whole world."

Obadiah nodded. "Good. Means you're worthy of carrying it."

Bill watched the horizon until stars filled the sky as Obadiah rode off alone into the good night.

This story is dedicated to unconquerable Sam Steele of the North-West Mounted Police, who really did leave Crowfoot's teepee with his prisoner in tote.

Texas Ranger Wes Crowley and the Bank Robber

HARVEY STANBROUGH

Newly sworn-in Texas Rangers Dramon and Siler were waiting on the boardwalk in front of the Amarillo Inn for their corporals to come out. They had both taken the oath a few days earlier. Today, Corporals Wes Crowley and Otis "Mac" McFadden were going to run them through their paces on the shooting range west of town.

Both corporals and the other more seasoned Rangers had all spent a little time with the two newbies. In turns, the older Rangers had given Dramon and Siler tips on several things a Ranger needs to know: everything from how to build a bedroll, to what should always be ready to go in your possibles bag, to which women to avoid over at Miss Abigail's Home for Wayward Young Women.

Wes came out of the Amarillo Inn first.

Siler only nodded.

Dramon grinned. "Mornin', Corporal Crowley."

Wes nodded. "Mornin'." He walked past the young men and stopped at the edge of the boardwalk, looking west down the street.

A long moment ago, from the window in his room on the second floor of the Inn, he'd seen a man he thought he recognized.

As Mac came out of the Inn, Wes looked away for a moment and blinked his eyes, then looked down the street again.

The man wasn't there.

Mac looked over the two new Rangers as he pulled the door shut behind him. "You boys all set to go?"

Both men were dressed similarly in pants and off-white shirts, no collars, boots, hats, and a gun belt. Each man wore a Colt revolver in a holster on his right hip, and each man was carrying a Winchester carbine in his left hand.

Dramon, wide-eyed, blond, and lanky at around six feet with a slight, wiry build, nodded and grinned. “Yes sir.”

Siler nodded too. He was about the same height, with thick, dark brown hair and a darker complexion than most Anglos. He seemed to wear a serious look most of the time.

Mac glanced past them at Wes. “Is he still down there?”

Wes turned around and shook his head. “Naw.”

“Well, I just wanted you to know I was ready.” A grin tugged at the corner of Mac’s mouth. Then he looked at the boys again. “You have your bedrolls an’ your possibles bags down at the livery stable, do you?”

Dramon frowned and glanced at Siler, then back at Mac. “No sir. We’re only goin’ to the shootin’ range, right?”

“Yeah, but a long time ago a buddy of mine taught me a valuable lesson. You’re Rangers now, so always be ready to go into action.”

Dramon nodded. “Yes sir.”

But Mac wasn’t through. “Now what do you suppose would happen if we get out there, an’ right in the middle of your trainin’, one of the other Rangers rides out to get us ‘cause half the Comanche nation decided to raid Amarillo? An’ just as we come ridin’ in, the Indians light out to the east?”

Dramon’s eyes were wide. “Sir, I don’t—”

“Well, I’ll tell you what would happen. The rest of us would be hot on their trail, but you boys couldn’t go. You’d have to stop off here to get your bedrolls an’ your possibles bags first. See? So anytime you get on your horse to leave town, outfit yourself to be gone for a few days. You never know.”

“Yes sir,” Dramon said. “So should we go get our stuff?”

“Yeah, go ahead. We’ll wait.”

As the two younger men went back into the Amarillo Inn, Mac glanced at Wes. "Come to think of it, I'm gonna go back up an' get a canteen. You need anything from your room?"

"Nah, I'm good. I'll wait out here."

As Mac went inside, Wes thought about the man he'd seen from his window. He looked down the street again.

Still nothing. *Maybe I didn't recognize him. Maybe it was just a guy waiting for a friend.* He muttered, "Or maybe he was just a figment of my imagination."

As he ran the face against possible matches among his memories, Wes decided to head toward the livery stable. The others would catch up soon enough.

As he started along the boardwalk he thought about Dramon and Siler. They're so young, so idealistic. He grinned. *I thought Dramon was gonna pass out when Mac asked him about his bedroll and possibles bag.*

He thought about all the other young Rangers he and Mac had put through their paces on the range over the past several years. Probably a dozen or so, and they all had that one thing in common: they were as green as could be, but they thought they were worldly.

He chuckled and shook his head. *I wonder if me and Mac looked that green when Connolly and Stanton took us to the range all those years ago?*

Without realizing it, he was halfway to the livery stable. *Come to think of it, we might'a been even greener than these two boys.* As he stepped into the street, he glanced to his right. There was the corner where the man was standing earlier, then the milliner, then the bank. *Me an' Mac were only sixteen an'—*

Across the street, the front door of the bank shoved open and slapped against the wall. Three men backed out onto the boardwalk, their guns drawn. One of them said, "You folks just keep your mouth shut an'—"

Wes crouched and turned, his Colt suddenly in his hand and cocked. He said, "Stop, gents. You twitch an' I'll shoot you dead."

The man on the right spun around and leveled his revolver.

Wes's Colt bucked with an explosion and the man slammed backward into a chair next to the door, then crumpled face-down to the boardwalk. Blood spatter stained the back of the chair and the wall.

Wes straightened from his crouch and started toward the other two men. *Better to be on the same side of the street. I don't need a wagon or a horse to come between me and them.*

The other two quickly turned around, their hands raised and still holding the guns, and their eyes huge.

One of them said, "Don't shoot, mister!"

Wes stopped a few feet from the boardwalk. He looked the men over, but neither of them was the man he'd seen before. One was far too young, though he seemed to resemble the earlier man. The other was in his mid-thirties to early forties.

Wes gestured with his Colt. "Toss them hoglegs out here in the street."

The one who had asked Wes not to shoot immediately tossed his gun into the street.

But a surly look crossed the other man's face. "This is a good revolver. I ain't fixin' to drop it in the dirt." He sneered. "I'd be more'n happy to *hand* it to you though."

The younger man looked at the older one. "Ross, he's a Texas Ranger! You can't—"

The surly man said, "Shut up, boy."

Wes shrugged and purposely cocked his Colt. The sound was crisp. It almost echoed. "Mister, it makes no difference to me. Mine's already cocked an' leveled. Now, you can toss that thing easy if you want to." His voice quieted. "Or, if you're sure, you can move in any other way at all. But if you do that, I guarantee that 'good revolver' will drop out of your dead hand."

The man looked at him for a moment, very careful not to move, then nodded almost imperceptibly and tossed the revolver into the street. When it landed, a small puff of dust went up.

From behind Wes, Mac said, "Damn, Crowley, you *are* impressive when you're pissed off."

Never taking his gaze off the men, Wes nodded. "Whatever you say, Mac." Then he gestured with the Colt again. "Now, you two turn back around an' put your hands as high as you can get 'em on that wall."

From beside Mac, Dramon whispered, "Corporal McFadden, shouldn't we help him or somethin'?"

Grinning, Mac shook his head. Quietly, he said, "Does he *look* like he needs any help? Just watch."

The would-be bank robbers had turned around. As they put their palms against the wall, the surly one said, "A'right, now what?"

Wes said, "Well, now all you gotta do is stay right there 'til I tell you different."

"Yeah, well, that don't really fit in too well with my plans. I was gonna—"

Wes stepped up on the boardwalk and dug the barrel of his Colt into the man's side. "Shut up, friend. I'm tired of listenin' to you talk."

Mr. Peabody, the banker, rushed through the door of the bank. He was a thin, mousey little man in a three-piece brown tweed suit. He'd left his hat inside and a few strands of hair were blowing in the wind, occasionally slapping his balding head. He gaped at the two men, then looked at Wes. He sounded flustered. "Thank goodness you happened along, Corporal Crowley! Thank goodness at least *some* of the lawmen in this town are doing their job." He swung one arm around and pointed an accusing finger at Wes' captives. "These men *just this very minute* were—"

The surly one turned his head and sneered. "Shut up, runt, or I'll come back to visit you as soon as—"

Wes clocked the man alongside the head with the barrel of his Colt.

The man crumpled like a pole-axed steer.

Wes glanced down. "I tried to tell you, mister."

Still in the street, Mac grinned at Dramon and Siler. Quietly, he said, "See what I mean?"

Mr. Peabody tried again. "As I was *trying* to say, just a moment ago these *very* men were involved in robbing my—"

"Yes sir, Mr. Peabody, I understand." Wes gestured for the banker to calm down. He holstered his Colt. "It's all right. I know what they did. Listen, would you do me a favor? Would you mind goin' down the street to get the sheriff for me?"

"I *suppose* I can do that, given that he should already be here."

Wes looked at him, his eyes flat. "You've got the best sheriff in the whole panhandle. Now, could you go on ahead an' get him for me?"

The banker paled. "Ri-right away, sir." And he hurried off.

Wes mumbled, "I sure wish he wouldn't call me sir. Makes me feel all itchy." He glanced back at Mac and the two young Rangers with him. "Ya'll just gonna stand there an' let me do all the work?" Without waiting for an answer, he turned around and moved over next to the man he'd shot, crouched, and lifted the man's shoulder so he could see his face.

Not the man I saw before.

He straightened and looked at the last remaining upright would-be bank robber. "All right, you. Turn around for me."

The man turned around, but he kept his hands high. He was young, probably in his late teens or early twenties.

"Seems like you got more sense than these other two combined. What's your name?"

"Josey, sir. Josey Boyle Talbot."

Wes frowned. "Talbot. That name sounds familiar. Do I know you?"

"No sir, prob'ly not, but I remember *you* well enough."

Wes crossed his arms. "Is that right? From where?"

"You came to my uncle's house. You an' another Ranger." The young man glanced in Mac's direction, then pointed. "That big guy, he was with you. It was just after the Comanches raided our place. I was only seven back then. Me an' my daddy, we was visitin' my uncle an' my aunt, an'—"

"That's up in the northwest corner of the state, right? I mean almost *smack* in the corner?"

"Yes sir. My uncle's farm. On the other side of Dalton."

"An' what's your daddy's name?"

"Jude Talbot. Well, Judas, but he goes by Jude. I mean, he *went* by Jude. He used to be a preacher." He hesitated. "'Least that's what he said. When I knew him he was a farm hand most of the time. We... well, we traveled around a lot."

Wes said, "All right, an' where is he right now?"

"I— I'm sorry. He ain't here. He was killed that day. That day when the Comanches came."

Wes nodded. "All right. That's right. I remember now. He was the man by the well, wasn't he?"

"Yes sir. That's where I saw him when you Rangers came ridin' up."

Wes looked at the boardwalk for a moment, then looked up again and frowned. "So what I'm tryin' to figure out, Josey, is what are you doin' here?"

The young man frowned. "I'm— well, I mean, I *was*— I mean, we were—" He gestured with his head at the men on the ground. "Me an' them guys, we were robbin'—"

"No, I know what you were doin' *here*. I meant why are you even involved? You don't seem the kind to hang out with these guys. You tellin' me you've done this before? That you're part of this gang of desperados here?" Sarcasm dripped from his voice as he gestured loosely toward the men lying on the boardwalk.

"Oh, no sir. No *sir*. This was my first time. What I mean, this was my *only* time. I ain't gonna do it again, that's for sure."

Wes nodded. "Well, six of one, half a dozen of the other." He thought for a moment. "Who raised you, Josey?"

"My uncle, sir."

Wes nodded. "An' he was at the farm that day too, was he?"

"Yes sir. They killed my pa, an'—"

Wes snapped his fingers. "Wait. Isn't your uncle's name Josey too?"

"No sir. They called him Josey though. Mostly my aunt Mary called him Josey, but that was short for Joseph Wesley. Anyway, nowadays he goes by JW. The Indians... they killed my aunt. My pa had me hidin' back underneath the porch."

"An' then your uncle raised you after that?"

"Yes sir. I think they would'a found him an' me too an' killed us both if they'd have stayed. B-but it's like they knew you were comin'. They weren't gone very long before you got there."

Wes nodded. "Yeah, I remember." He looked over his shoulder. "Remember, Mac? We saw their dust cloud as they rode out."

Mac only nodded.

Wes looked at the boy again. "An' your uncle, he's here in town too, ain't he?"

"Yes sir. Well, he was. After he told the others where to meet up with him, he left."

Wes glanced back at Mac again. "That's who I saw this mornin'." He turned back to the kid. "He told ya'll where to meet up? So this bank robbery, this was *his* idea?"

Josey looked at the boardwalk. "Yes sir."

Wes frowned. "But ain't he a farmer?"

"No sir. Not no more. Not for a long time. After they killed Aunt Mary, he changed."

Wes nodded. "Yeah, well. Things like that'll change a man for sure." Wes paused and frowned.

"But it's okay with him that *you're* doin' this?"

The young man looked up, his eyes wide. "Oh, no sir. *No* sir. He don't know. I came down here with him, but he didn't know I heard him an' the others talkin'. After he lit out this mornin', I came in an' told 'em I wanted in on it too." He hesitated and looked down. "It—it seemed like it'd be excitin'."

"Yeah, well, you're right about that. An' I guess you see how excitin' it can be." Wes gestured toward the dead man. "You see what you can get now too, don't you? An' how quick you can get it."

"Yes sir."

"An' you're sure you ain't gonna leave here an' go find an easier place to rob? Maybe one where there ain't a Texas Ranger on every street corner?"

"No. No *sir*. Fact is, I'd rather be like you."

Wes nodded. "Well, now that ain't much to aspire to. How old are you right now?"

"I'll be twenty-one in a few months."

"All right." Wes gestured, trying to calm the boy down. "All right. Tell you what, for now you're gonna stay with the sheriff for awhile. I need some time to think. Maybe I can figure out some way to help you, all right? But don't you give the sheriff no trouble. An' when Big Mouth here wakes up," and he nudged the man he'd cold-cocked with the toe of his boot, "you steer clear of this'n, understand? 'Cause that's one ol' boy who ain't gonna change his stripes. They run too deep."

"Yes sir. I won't have nothin' to do with any of 'em anymore."

Mr. Peabody came huffing up with the sheriff. "I tried to tell him to hurry, Corporal, but he just wouldn't."

The sheriff stepped past Peabody, grinned, and extended his hand. "How you doin', Wes?" He glanced at the young man on the boardwalk, then down at the other two. "Doin' my job for me again I see."

"Well, it wasn't quite like that, Sheriff Porter. These morons kind'a backed into my lap." He pointed at the dead one. "That one decided to test me when I said if they moved I'd shoot 'em."

The sheriff nodded. "I'm seein' that he failed the test." With the toe of his boot, he prodded the right calf of the other one who was lying on the boardwalk. "What this one's problem?"

"That'n's Ross somethin' or other. The kid can fill you in proper. Ol' Ross was runnin' off at the mouth an' I ran short of patience. Seemed to me he wanted really bad to shut up but he couldn't figure out how to do it, so I helped him out. He'll prob'ly have a pretty good knot on the side of his head for a day or two."

The sheriff pointed at Josey. "And this one?"

"He's a special case. Put him in a cell by himself if you would. I don't want him locked up with this idiot. I'll need to talk with Mr. Peabody, see what kind'a role he had in this deal if any, an' then do some thinkin'. I might talk the judge into givin' him a choice, joinin' the Rangers or the army or goin' to jail." He raised one hand and gestured as if he was turning a key, then extended three fingers.

The sheriff nodded, then grinned and emitted a quiet whistle. "I don't know about that first choice. At least in jail or the army you get two hot meals a day an' a regular place to sleep." He laughed. "I'll take care of it." He looked around at Mac and the two younger men, each wearing a Ranger badge. He shook his head. Quietly he said, "Ya'll headin' out to the range?"

Mac nodded.

The sheriff looked at Wes again. "Man, they're gettin' younger all the time." He frowned. "And where are Rob Corazol and Will Granger? I thought they were doin' most of the trainin' these days?"

"They're supposed to be on their way back from Austin. I'm just hopin' they'll be back before we have to head out on the next patrol." Wes grinned. "Oh, and as far as talkin' about 'em gettin' younger, these two are both a few years older than Mac and I were."

The sheriff shook his head. "Ain't that something."

Wes said, "Well, we'd best get on out to the range. This little deal cost us a good fifteen minutes of ridin' time."

The sheriff grinned. "See you later, Wes. An' thanks."

Wes waved and stepped off the boardwalk to approach Mac, Dramon and Siler.

The sheriff turned and looked into the crowd that had gathered. He pointed. "John, you an' Bill there grab this guy an' carry him down to my office." He looked at Mr. Peabody. "Could you send one of your tellers to get the undertaker for this ol' boy?" He gestured toward the inert form with his boot.

Mr. Peabody nodded. "Certainly, Sheriff. Right away."

"Thanks." The sheriff took Josey by the arm. "C'mon, son, let's go see how you like our accommodations."

***

Several minutes later Wes, Mac, Billy Dramon and Tom Siler were riding west from the livery stable.

Not long after they got outside of town, Wes looked at Mac. "Did you hear that boy back there? He remembers us from that raid up northwest of Dalton. His pa and his aunt were killed, an' he an' his uncle survived. The uncle was a farmer. Now I guess he's an outlaw."

"Yeah I remember that one. That was what, about ten, twelve years ago?"

"Thirteen, I guess. Kid says he was seven an' he's almost twenty-one now."

Mac nodded. "That was the first raid after Watson where we almost caught up to ol' Four Crows. At least he didn't have time to finish the job."

Wes shook his head. "Watson. Man that was a good idea. We came so close. An' then for awhile, we didn't know what was goin' on with that crazy Comanche, remember? It was like he disappeared."

Mac laughed. "As I recall, he disappeared a lot over the years. But yeah, I think that was the first big time. The first time that made us hope he wasn't comin' back."

Ranger Dramon said, "Corporal Crowley, what was that thing you did back there?"

"What thing?"

"After you told the sheriff to lock up the younger one, you did something with your hand then raised three fingers."

Mac laughed.

Wes grinned. "I don't believe he's a bad boy. I think he just woke up and decided to do something stupid. He heard what I said about talkin' to the judge an' all that. But that 'thing' I did was my signal to the sheriff. He'll hold him for three days an' probably put the fear of god into him. But after that he'll let him go."

Dramon shook his head, and they all broke into a canter.

Howl

LONDON BAKER

Pa and I stood, gazing down at the mangled sheep in front of us. Their legs were twisted up like the gnarled branches of a tree, eyes hollow and glossed over. I looked up at Pa, watched the way his jaw twitched as he stared out over the flat stretch of waist-high grass that surrounded our home.

"What do you think got 'em?" I asked.

He didn't answer. His eyes stayed trained ahead, the faint stubble dotting his cheeks adding darkness to the shadow cast on him by the rising sun. After a moment, he faced me. "Go get your Mama, boy."

"Yes, sir," I replied, darting off back towards the clapboard shack we called home.

There were four of us right now, one more on the way. There was me, Pa, Mama, Aggie, and the baby. As I walked I could feel a chill in the air, like the summer was toying with us as it slid away. Inside, Mama was crouched over the hearth, tending to the fire.

"Mama?" I said.

She turned, "What is it, Will?"

"Pa told me to come in and get you. Somethin' got the sheep."

Mama put her hand to her face as she stood, "God help us."

I watched her walk towards the open front door, noting the way that she limped. Her stomach stuck out so far now, the baby was probably only weeks away. With her hand on the door, Mama turned to me, "Go get your sister and take her down to the river."

"Aw Ma—"

She raised her eyebrow and I let my voice trail off. Maybe I was fourteen, but that didn't matter to her. As far as she was concerned I'd be eight years old forever. Kicking my feet, using one heel to wipe dust off of the other, I replied, "Yes ma'am."

I paused for a moment before heading to the bedroom Aggie and I shared. I wanted to listen, to hear what Mama had to say to Pa, what he would tell her about the things that got the sheep. I was scared, real scared, and I couldn't even say why.

Aggie had her back to me as I leaned up against the doorframe, the light from the open window only slightly illuminating the space. She held a paper doll in her hand and was making it jump over a rock she'd brought inside the day before.

"Aggie," I said, my voice loud in the morning stillness.

She jumped, "Will! You scared me."

"C'mon Aggie, Mama says we got to go down and play in the river."

"But *whyyy*," her voice whined. Sometimes I forgot she was only six.

"Mama said so."

Aggie pouted, "Why do you always do everything she tells you."

"C'mon Aggie," I held my hand out to her.

Reluctantly, she stood, tucking the doll into her bed. As she reached up, I realized how much my hand engulfed hers, how it swallowed hers so there was nothing left. "Where's Pa?" Aggie asked.

"He and Mama are having a meetin'," I replied, purposefully leaving out the sheep. No need to scare her.

She looked thoughtful for a moment, but I could soon see dismissal wash over. I envied that, marveled at the way she was able to let things flow off of her like raindrops on a window. Me, I couldn't. I couldn't let things slide. There was no way to forget these types of things.

"This way," I said, leading her through the tall brush.

Up ahead I could just see the haphazardly compiled roofs of our neighbor's home, fellow pioneers and families who had not the strength to plow further West. The solution? Set up camp here, build a life for ourselves.

The river's voice was a dull roar, like a quiet predator crouched low in the bushes. It gurgled, a bawl or bellow, a thunderous echo traipsing across the sandy plains and into our ears. We'd been lucky to find the river, lucky that it'd been here. If it hadn't, who knows what would've become of us.

Aggie ran ahead, her dress trailing in the dust around her feet. The river lolled over rocks, small droplets spraying upwards and allowing a fine mist to drift over the surrounding plants. Aggie had thrown off her shoes and now jumped ankle deep in the cool waters.

"Hey, Will."

I turned around. Billy stood behind me, his red hair blown every which way by the wind. Freckles dotted his face like bullet holes, his eyes twinkled impishly. "Hey."

"Your Mama make you take her out here?" Billy asked, gesturing with his head towards Aggie.

"Yup," I grabbed him by the arm, leading him just out of earshot. Glancing back I made sure Aggie was still visible. "Somethin' got our sheep."

"Are you joshing?" Billy raised an eyebrow.

"No, I promise. Pa and I went out this morning and they were all bloodied up. I could see their guts hanging out."

"Wow! You guys know what got 'em?"

"Nope, not a clue."

"I'll bet I do," Billy said, grinning smugly.

"No you don't," I said, grinning right back.

A storm flashed across his face, "I'll bet I do, Will. I'll bet it was a Wailer."

I could feel the smile drain from my face, "A what?"

"You heard me," Billy's voice was low, "a Wailer."

"Wha...what's that?" I asked, not sure if I really wanted to know.

"You've never heard about the Wailers?"

I shook my head, "Ain't ever heard of no such thing."

For some reason we both turned to look at Aggie. She stood knee deep now, chucking small stones across the river to the opposite bank. Billy leaned in, his voice nearly imperceptible above the monotone sound of rushing water, "The Wailers are ghosts, real ones, not like the ones your Pa tells us about 'round the fire."

"Ghosts?"

Billy nodded solemnly, "Yep. They're the spirits of settlers that didn't make it. At night they walk around, wailing and crying out because they want to go West. They'll kill anything in their paths. That's probably what—"

I clapped my hands over my ears, "Stop it Billy, stop!"

Billy shrugged, "Don't say I didn't warn you."

We stood side-by-side for a moment. Billy was staring off at the town, while my eyes were trained on Aggie. Again I felt that stab of envy. There she was playing innocently, not a clue about what was going on. And then there was me, stuck over here, trying not to think about the Wailers.

"Say, Billy..." I hesitated.

"Yeah?" Billy crooked an eyebrow expectantly.

"If I did believe all that—you know—that the Wailers killed the sheep, what then?"

Billy's face darkened, "Well then I'd say you'd better be worried. *Really* worried."

"Why?" I asked.

"'Cause they'll come for you next," a cloudy smile played on his lips. "They'll take your Mama, your Pa, and even Aggie."

Despite the early afternoon sunlight I felt cold, like someone had taken a handful of snow and dropped it down the back of my shirt without me even noticing. Would they *actually* come for me? For my family?

"It happened to Sam Godwin once," Billy added.

"Who?"

"Sam Godwin. The Wailers took him and his whole family too."

I ran a hand through my hair, "What if they...what if they come for me?"

Billy crossed his arms smugly, "I thought you didn't even believe in 'em."

"Say I did," I said quickly, "is there anything that can stop them?"

Billy nodded, "The Wailers sleep during the day. You gotta kill 'em while they're sleeping."

"Where do they sleep?"

Billy pointed, gesturing away from town towards where grass bled into forest, "Out there."

"So what do we do?"

"We hunt."

I looked back over at Aggie. "I'd have to take her home first."

Billy gazed around, glancing up towards the sky, then towards the town, out towards the plains, and then finally back at me, "Let's meet here after supper."

"Alright," I replied.

I waved and walked towards Aggie.

***

Supper consisted of a thick soup, as well as bread baked over the hearth. The aroma had greeted Aggie and I as we tramped back from the river, both of us cracking smiles of delight. Pa had cleared the sheep out, but I could still imagine them. I could still see the blood and smell the awful stench.

I told Mama I was going out to play with Billy. She looked over at Pa who nodded. Finally, turning to me, she said, "Fine, just be home before dark."

"Yes, ma'am," I had no intention of being out any later than that, especially with the Wailers around.

I was halfway out the door when Pa's voice stopped me, "Son?"

"Yes?"

He sounded exhausted, "Be careful."

"I will, Pa."

And with that I was free, my legs springing out in front of me as I charged through the grass. The wind whipped my hair back, my heart thrummed wildly. I gulped the fresh air like soil does water after a drought.

Soon the sound of the rushing water met my ears. Billy was reclined on the trunk of a tree, head resting against the bark. He nodded when he saw me, "'Bout time you showed up."

"Oh be quiet," I said. "You ready?"

Solemnly Billy stood, walking off into the vast expanse of the prairie. I followed him. The sun was just starting to sink. Soon, we'd be out of time. If the Wailers really were hiding out wherever Billy thought they were, then the last thing we needed was to stumble upon them right as they awoke.

The grass pricked at our legs, tall tendrils of yellow grasping out from the ground. It was as if the grass itself were alive, clutching at our calves and ankles as we wound our way through. I kept my eyes trained on the ground, "Are we getting close?"

Billy shook his head, "Just a little longer."

The forest blossomed up ahead of us, trees jutting up into the pale expanse of the mid-evening sky. It was hard to see between the trees, as if the inside of the forest was a land of shadow, as if we were walking towards some *other* universe.

Billy stopped at the forest's edge, "They're in there."

"The Wailers?"

Billy nodded. I took an extra step forward, the air cooler under the shade of the trees. Goosebumps broke out along my arms, my eyes attempted in vain to adjust to the dimness. The trunks of the trees were thick and I guessed that it would be impossible for me to even wrap my arms all the way around it.

"Will, come back here."

I glanced behind me. Without even realizing it I had drawn away from Billy, leaving him standing alone at the edge of the treeline. I hurried back towards him. There was something enchanting about the timberland, something that pulled me in. I turned to look at Billy, "What do we do if we find them?"

"We use this," Billy said, reaching into his pocket and pulling out his slingshot.

"A slingshot?" I almost laughed.

"It may not seem like much," Billy replied, "but I promise it works."

"And if it doesn't work" I demanded, "what then?"

"It will work," Billy said with a firmness I'd never heard from him before. He spoke with the power of my Pa, spoke with total confidence in his abilities.

"I trust you, Billy," I replied.

We plunged into the shadows walking shoulder to shoulder. The temperature was significantly cooler and I couldn't help but shiver. My heart leapt with every sound, my eyes darted towards every shifting shadow, every slight movement. Neither of us dared to speak. There was something sacred in the stillness.

A piercing howl broke the silence.

Billy and I shot a glance at one another and I prepared myself to run. Billy leaned in, his voice hardly a whisper in my ear, "We have to keep going."

I took a deep breath. "Okay."

It took everything in me not to run. Every time the impulse rose I thought of the sheep and how they'd been left strewn, a mangled mess. I thought about my Mama, my Pa, and of course Aggie. I thought of how I could never let what had happened to the sheep happen to them.

"Will," Billy breathed, "do you hear that?"

"What are you—"

I stopped mid-sentence. I *could* hear something. Craning my ears I listened intently into the darkness, as if willing my hearing to wrap around trees and sift through the fallen pine needles that blanketed the forest floor.

Another howl.

We again made eye contact, ducking low into a crouch. I was silently grateful for the pine needles and the way they blanketed our steps. Up ahead I could just make out the sound of rustling mixed with something else...what was it...

Heavy breathing.

Up ahead.

Something was panting up ahead, or rather multiple somethings.

Heaving, deep, gasping breaths.

Billy heard it too. Every step we took—all hunched over the way we were—was one step closer to the things up ahead. Was it the Wailers? A part of me hoped it was, hoped it was so that we could take them out. But another part of me prayed it wasn't.

Up ahead the trees parted to reveal a small clearing. I raised a hand to my mouth, stifling a gag, "What's that smell?"

"That's horrible," Billy whispered back.

We were right up against the treeline. One more shuffling step and we'd be in the clearing, along with whatever was making that stench. That rancid, putrid stench. The rustling noises were louder. It sounded like a whole village moving around, dozens of feet stomping on the ground.

"What do we do?" I hissed.

The sun was nearly invisible now, a faint red streak in the placid sky. Billy looked up, his head turning slowly to take in the surroundings. For a moment he was lost in thought. Finally, Billy leaned in, "We go home for the night."

"But what if they come back?" I demanded, still keeping my voice low. "What if they come for my family? For me or for Aggie?"

"Listen Will, we can't take on all of those things at once, at least not yet."

"So we—"

He cut me off, "Yes, we come back tomorrow."

I was about to reply when I noticed the silence.

Everything had fallen silent.

No more panting, no more shuffling of feet on the ground. The entire forest seemed to be holding its breath. There was no time to hesitate. I turned to Billy, "*Run*!"

We sprung to our feet and took off, legs carrying us like deer over logs and rocks, around trees and through the bramble. For a moment I could hear things crashing behind us, branches snapping, the sound of feet hammering after us.

But almost as soon as I first noticed it, it was gone. Whatever was back there had given up its pursuit. Billy and I didn't stop, though. We kept running until the treeline faded into the distance behind us. We ran until the sound of the river was louder than our heavy breathing.

"I...I...I think we can stop now," Billy panted.

I nodded, too short of breath to add anything else. I was in awe at how fast life had changed. This very morning Billy and I had stood next to this very river, whispering nonsense about dead sheep and Wailers. Only...it hadn't been nonsense. It had been real, it was real. There really was something in the woods.

"Should I tell my Pa?" I asked.

Billy thought for a moment, "Yeah, I think so."

"Meet back here tomorrow morning?"

Billy nodded, "Yep."

The words "*if we make it to tomorrow*" hung in the air, but neither of us dared to pluck them, to taste of the fruit that they would bear. By not saying them we were shining light into the darkness. We *would* make it to tomorrow, we *would* survive the night.

"See you then," I said, turning to walk back home.

"Bye, Will," he replied, trudging in the opposite direction.

I half-walked, half-ran. I didn't want to be outside any longer than I had to. I wasn't ashamed to admit that, every few moments, I'd cast a glance over my shoulder. That horrible breathing noise kept playing in my head, banging around like an echo in a cave. I couldn't seem to shake it. I couldn't get that awful stench out of my nose either.

Pa was standing near the woodpile, axe poised above his head. He sent it crashing down, severing a log in two. He looked up when he heard me approach, "You have fun?"

"Yes, sir."

I stood by him, watching as he halved another log. There were so many things I wanted to say, so many words brimming. I knew that if I opened my mouth they would cascade out, a heavy waterfall of thoughts and fears streaming their way down my face and towards him.

But I couldn't say anything, I couldn't. What would he think of his son, too scared to even fight back against those things? He'd be so ashamed of me. Pa split another log and glanced over, "Something bothering you, son?"

"No, Pa. Nothing's bothering—"

"Will," Pa said, his voice stern, "I raised you to tell no lies."

"Yeah, I know, but—"

Pa set the axe down and placed a calloused hand on my shoulder, "Listen, here. There's no 'but' that makes up for telling a lie. Nothin' that justifies not bringing the truth out. The truth's a beast. You keep it locked up and eventually it rips itself out. It's always messier that way too."

"I know what got the sheep, Pa."

He raised an eyebrow, "What did you see son?"

"Wailers, Pa," I stammered. "Billy called 'em Wailers."

"Wailers? I'm not sure I understand," Pa ran a hand through his thinning hair.

"They're like ghosts or monsters or something. Like the demons we hear about in church," I replied.

"And you saw these where?"

Now that I'd started I couldn't stop, "Out in the forest. I told Billy this mornin' about the sheep so we went out lookin' for what took them. We went on in the forest, and came to this clearing. It smelled awful, Pa. Like rot or something. Then we heard these noises, like feet shuffling or creatures breathing. We took off then. Billy and I hadn't thought there'd be as many as we heard, we thought there'd be maybe two or three at the most. Anyways, when we ran away we could hear them chasing us and—"

"These 'Wailers' were chasing you?" Pa asked.

"Yes, sir. They chased us and we ran all the way to the river before we thought it was safe to stop. Billy said they got Sam Godwin and his family."

"Sam who?"

"Godwin," I answered.

"I ain't ever heard of no one named Godwin, but you're certain *you* heard something? Certain you smelled something?" Pa asked.

"Yes, Pa. I promise. I wouldn't kid about something like this."

Pa stared off for a moment, his hand running over the dark stubble on his face. I'd seen that expression earlier, when we'd gone out this morning and found the sheep. After a moment, he turned to face me, "Tomorrow I want you to take me there, to show me what you saw. For tonight, I want you to sleep."

"What if they come back?" I asked, my voice shaking and giving away more of my fear than I'd wanted to.

"Then I will protect us," Pa said, bringing his hand to my head and messing up my hair.

"Promise?"

He smiled, wrinkles spreading across his face like ripples on the surface of a pond in the twilight shadow, "I promise."

I slept well that night, better than I had in ages. My mind kept thinking back to what my Pa said, how he said he'd protect us. I thought about my Mama too. Maybe sometimes Mama treated me like I was a little baby, but for tonight I didn't mind it. I didn't mind that I was loved or that this place was warm. Tomorrow we would go out and Pa would kill the Wailers.

But for tonight we all would sleep.

***

Pa shook me awake. The sun barely poked through the windows, thin beams slicing across the dusty room. He leaned in and whispered. I could smell fresh coffee on his breath, "Let's go, son."

I slunk out of bed and slipped into my clothes, doing everything in my power to shut the door to the bedroom gently. No need to wake Aggie. Pa was pouring another cup of coffee by the fireplace. When he saw me he stood, holding the enamel mug out to me. I took it, hesitating for a moment, "I thought I wasn't supposed to have none 'till I was grown."

Pa smiled, his voice still a whisper, "This mornin' you can. You did the right thing coming to me, you know that? Would've been awfully stupid doin' this just you and Billy."

I took a slow sip from the mug, the black coffee bitter on my tongue. There was a hint of some spice, an almost smoky quality to it. I took another big gulp. Pa placed his heavy hand on my shoulder, "Ready?"

"Yes, sir."

We plunged out into the still morning, me clutching my coat tightly over my frame. A thin mist clung to the undergrowth and Pa stomped forward, carving a path through it. He had an unloaded shotgun thrown over his shoulders and I carried the shells in my pocket.

The din of the river filled the air and after a moment Pa asked, "So Billy will meet us down by the river?"

In answer to his question Billy's voice rose up over the rushing waters, "Morning Will! Morning Mister Barkley!"

Pa smiled, but his eyes were hard. Sleep played at the corners. And something else too. Could it be fear? Pa spoke loudly enough to be heard over the river, "Good morning, Billy."

Silence fell upon us as we pressed together, Pa towering over us. Wordlessly we began to walk through the knee-high grass, weaving our way towards where the trees jutted out from the ground. Soon we stood at the edge of the forest, the early twilight shadows of last night having vanished with the rising sun.

Pa scratched his head, "So these...what were they again?"

"Wailers," Billy replied.

"Right," Pa said, "so these Wailers, they live in here?"

"Yeah," I answered, "in a clearing. They were eating something."

We began to walk through the forest, pine needles cushioning our steps. Billy and I peered around every tree, silently praying there would be nothing behind them. Our hearts pounded like drums, sweat broke out on my forehead.

"The clearing's right up ahead, Mister Barkley," Billy said.

"Will," Pa said, not looking at me.

"Yes, sir?"

"Can you hand me the shells?"

I passed him five shotgun shells and he loaded one into the gun, sliding the others into his pocket. He racked the gun with a satisfying click. The clearing was up ahead. Just a few more steps and we would be in it.

Pa had the gun pointed forward, ready at any moment to apply pressure to the trigger. A branch cracked under my feet and I couldn't help but jump. There was a light breeze, gently blowing the boughs of the pine trees. The wind carried the rot, brought along the same putrid odor from the day before.

I noticed Pa's face wrinkle, as if by scrunching his visage he could block out the stink of death. He hefted the shotgun, and I noticed a line of sweat where his hand had been. We paused right outside the treeline of the clearing. The noises of yesterday were absent. All was still.

We stepped into the clearing.

Billy drew in a sharp breath.

Pa muttered a curse, something I'd never heard him do before.

I felt sweat bead and slip down my back.

Wolves.

At least ten of them. All asleep, pressed up against towering rocks, burrowed deep in the grass of the clearing. Bones and half-rotted carcasses were strewn around, the scattered remains of everything from deer to sheep to rabbit.

Pa put a finger to his lips, silently imploring us to *stay quiet.* We backed up slowly, one step at a time until the clearing vanished behind the thick brush of the woods. I opened my mouth to say something, but Pa shook his head.

We walked out of the woods in silence. I was afraid to even step on the pine needles for fear that the smallest sound might bring the wolves down upon us. Pa was the first to speak, "Well, boys, looks like you did find the vermin who killed our sheep. They certainly ain't ghosts, though."

"What'll we do about it?" I asked.

Pa smiled, "*We* won't do anything. I'll get a group from the town together and we'll ride out this afternoon."

"But Pa—"

He cut me off, "No 'buts' son."

"Can we go out too, Mister Barkley?" Billy asked.

Pa laughed out loud, "You've got to be kiddin' me. Absolutely not."

"We want to help, though," I began to plead. "We found 'em so we should be able to—"

"That's exactly right, Will. You guys found 'em. You've done your job. Adventure is all good fun until it's not, and it doesn't take much for the whole thing to cross over that line. Being stupid isn't bravery. Bravery was coming to get me, was telling me what you saw. What do you think would've gone down had you two tried to confront your 'Wailers' by yourself?"

"We'd be dead," I muttered.

"Exactly," Pa's voice boomed, echoing across the field as we walked towards town. "You'd both be dead. You've done more than enough. It's not your job to fix everything. Let me take over now. You both understand?"

"Yes, sir," Billy and I murmured in unison.

***

Pa assembled together the men of the village. They mounted horses and loaded shells into shotguns. Great clouds of dust kicked up off of the ground as they plunged towards the forest. Nature was beauty that they all believed needed to be preserved, but it was also the belief of these men that threats against our safety must be eradicated.

Billy and I stared after them, hearts yearning to join in. Yearning to mount a horse, to charge across the plain, to help avenge the livestock that had been killed. Pa had discovered it was not just their home that had been targeted, but numerous residents in the village.

The sound of gunshots echoed across the prairie and I glanced over to Billy. There would be no more dead sheep. All was safe now.

***

Pa returned that night, his shotgun slung over his shoulder. He seemed worn, looked older than I'd ever seen him. Aggie and Mama were asleep, but I'd sat up waiting for him. I wanted to hear about it, to hear about the exploits.

"Pa!" I exclaimed.

He smiled at me, "Shouldn't you be asleep?"

I laughed, "How did it go, Pa? Did you kill 'em all?"

Pa motioned for me to sit by the fire as he pulled a chair over, "Most of 'em, yes. But that's not the point, son. The point isn't the bloodshed or death, it's the protection it provides. I love wolves. They're beautiful creatures. They have families, kind of like us."

I nodded and Pa went on, "But it was a danger to keep them around, so we had to do something. You understand?"

"Yes, sir."

We were silent for a moment. A smile broke out across Pa's face, "I won't lie to you though, Will. It was pretty dang fun."

I laughed and he joined in. Heaving on the laughter, Pa reached into his pocket, "I almost forgot, I've got something for you."

Pa held out his hand. A sharp, canine tooth rested on the palm, the roots slightly bloody. I felt my heart begin to thrum as I reached out. I tightened my hand and felt the sharp point of the tooth bite into my palm.

"Keep it as a reminder," Pa said. "There are things in this world more powerful than you, but even great evil or danger can be overcome. Okay?"

"Yes, sir," I stammered. "Thank you."

He tousled my hair, "Now get some rest."

"Goodnight, Pa."

Pa smiled, "Goodnight."

I walked into the room Aggie and I shared, her gentle snoring a lulling enchantment pulling me off into the land of dreams and sleep. The moon was visible through the window, casting full light on the swaying grass. I slid into the covers, the blanket scratching at my legs.

The wolf's tooth was still clenched in my hand, and I held it up, letting the moonlight illuminate it. After a moment I set it on the bedside table. I vowed never to lose it.

It was then that I drifted off to sleep.

END

Greater Love Hath No Man

BRADY PUTZKE

The boy crouched low and ran a hand through the tangled brush. The scratchy feeling distracted from the hairs on the back of his neck standing on end. Some of the small branches were bent westward, and a man had done it—he knew somehow.

"Why they like this, Bill? Bent that aways?" The boy asked, pointing towards the afternoon sun and turning to the big man at his left.

"Kiowa. Marking path," answered Sheriff William Hensley. "Don't reckon it's one you'll wanna be following."

The boy, Elijah Anderson by name, felt an icy chill creep down his spine, the summer sun serving only to add more cold sweat to his tan cotton shirt. Elijah shivered and couldn't hide it.

"Nothin' to be worryin' over, son."

Elijah felt something knot up in his gut, being called that. Just a nickname, he knew, but it made him think of Pa. Of the War that was ending as he was bein' born. Of being lonely.

Bill looked down at him then, and 'Lijah didn't know one way or another if the Sheriff knew what he was thinking, but there was a look of something kind and caring in the older man's eyes. Bill tousled Elijah's shaggy brown hair a bit and cracked a small smile.

"Ye ever kill an Injun, Bill?"

"Don't figger that's something your Ma would much like me discussin' with ye, 'Lijah."

"And why not? I'm damn near a grown man now. I know 'bout death and such. Bout

fightin'."

"You'll watch yer mouth, bein' but thirteen, so's you don't go wanderin' round town cussin' like that an' gettin' Ol' Bill here in trouble with your Mama."

"What's she know 'bout anything?"

The Sheriff gave a light smack upside the boy's head. It didn't hurt him none but Elijah rubbed and mouthed an "ouch" for effect. Still, he couldn't hold back a grin.

"For first," Bill started, "she knows almighty more'n ye about death and fightin' and life or whatever ye was sayin' just there."

'Lijah just stared at his boots, felt his face somethin' hot. The Sheriff's little sermon got him thinking of Pa again.

"I didn't mean nothin', reckon," the boy said.

"Reckon not," Bill said. "Saddle up, son. Manner of speakin'."

"Wish we *was* still ridin', 'stead of bein' afoot," Elijah fairly whined.

"Hush up, now. Once we get our quarry, we'll be back to 'em. Not's like ye can ride a hoss for nothin' anyhow," Bill said, humor in his voice. Elijah smiled back.

Bill stood and the boy admired the broad frame, wiry but right tough, and tall. The face was scar-worn, bristle-shadowed and tan, but kind. Bill always was in his brown sack coat 'round town, but here giving lessons in huntin' and trackin' in this heat to poor little Elijah who didn't have no daddy -- and the boys in town never let him forget that — he was in his shirtsleeves, no lapel for that tin star, and 'Lijah could well imagine Bill thought him something like equal. But, after all, he was just a boy.

"Here." Bill pointed to a fresh track as he walked. "She's a big one."

The depression in the damp ground aside of the tributary was deep and 'Lijah knew 'nough to know that meant a large animal ahead.

"Only a few minutes this ways, if she's stopped for a drink," Bill said.

They pressed on for a spell, silent. "So..." Elijah trailed off.

"How's that?"

"You ever kill an Injun?"

Bill sighed. "Sometime a man's got to do some killing. That hour come upon me a few times."

"In the war?"

"Yeah. In the war. On the plains. Other times and places. I've been 'round a darn sight.

"Betcha din't mind much cussin' when ye was fightin' a war."

"Ye might listen to yer mama a bit more and learn there's a season for ev'ry thing under heaven, son."

"Mama read me from the Good Book. I know 'bout such things."

"Ye know almighty 'bout lots, it seems."

"Yeah, well I don' figger it mean much important, bein' thirteen. Lotta boys weren't much older'n me fought in that war."

"And a lot of them ain't come home from it."

A still silence washed over both of them then, both knowing what had been said without saying it. Everett Thomas Anderson, Pa, was no boy when he was fightin' for General Lee, but he sure was one that didn't come home. Elijah'd heard tell of his father, how he was a great man, but that was the only way'n which the boy knew his Pa. Everett T. Anderson was all stories and imagination. He weren't 'round no more, or was ever, to give sermons or tousle hair or give his boy a slap upside the head when he said something disrespectin' his mama.

"Ye know," Elijah started, ornery and intending to get under Bill's skin a bit, catch him in a hypocrisy (that big Bible word). "That same Good Book says 'Thou shalt not kill.'"

"I know a thing or two about the Law, son. Texas law and the Good Lord's."

"What's that s'posed to mean?"

"It means that same Book says there's a time to kill, too."

"And how's a body go 'bout knowin' when that is?" Elijah asked, doing his best to corner Bill again.

"Seek ye first the kingdom of God," Bill answered, seemingly nonsensical. "Ye can just say you ain't for knowin'."

Bill stopped suddenly. 'Lijah figured he'd gone in too hard on Bill and was gonna get hisself a whoopin' or another sermon, this one he bet more fiery than the last, but Bill simply pointed to his ear and made a shushing motion, pressing the other finger to his lips. Then Bill pointed two fingers to his eyes and then pointed forward with the same fingers and crouched behind a dogwood.

There by the stream was the deer, some forty yards off. A whitetail doe, dipping her head gingerly to the surface of the flowing water and lapping it gently. A gust stirred the willows and her head shot up, searching. It didn't seem she could see them two, Elijah having joined Bill behind the dense foliage.

"Lemme shoot," Elijah whispered.

Bill whipped his head around and the kindness he normally wore in his weathered face was replaced by wide-eyed rage. The glare said, "Pipe down, fool, you'll ruin the hunt."

The deer hadn't run. But she knew something was afoot.

Bill closed his eyes and moved his head and chest to indicate breathing through his nose, silently commanding Elijah to do the same. They waited ten or so breaths and the doe went back to drinking.

It turned broadside. Elijah knew this exposed a vital area behind the shoulder.

Bill lifted the Winchester in a smooth, practiced arc and thumbed the hammer to full-cock. He sighted the rifle. He exhaled halfway and squeezed.

CRACK!

The shot and clack-clack of Bill levering the action echoed through the trees and the bullet hit its mark. The doe jumped and then bolted for the brush.

"Watch her path, 'Lijah," Bill said, calm, focused.

Elijah made mental note of where the deer had run. They took a few more breaths and followed.

Thirty yards northeast they ran, the boy leading, and found her death-still on her side, eyes senseless glass globes. She looked sad and yet oddly peaceful.

It wasn't as if Elijah had never seen a dead deer but all this talk about war (and them knowing they was really talking about his Pa not coming home, being dead, and young boys being dead and not coming home) made this time different somehow. The knot in his gut was back.

"Thou shalt not kill," the boy muttered, eyes welling and hot shame flushing into his face because of it.

"That weren't about animals, son," Bill said.

"I know... I know. I mean.. I..."

"It's alright."

"I know," Elijah said, more firmly now. "I don't rightly know what I'm thinkin'."

Bill mussed the boy's hair again, chippered up his voice. "Let's head back aways and get them hosses. We'll haul 'er back into town."

"Alright," Elijah replied.

And they headed west to where they'd tied the roan and dapple.

***

Dusk falling on the little town, Elijah Anderson and Sheriff William Hensley, doe quarry in tow across the back of Bill's big roan, walked their horses past the sun-bleached false fronts of Nelly's Saloon, the General Store that belonged to old man Withers, Maggie's boarding house, and the livery stable that doubled infrequently as stage stop. The near rancid smell of frying lard from the boarding house kitchen wafted on the slightly cooling evening air, mixing sickly and sour with the scent of horse and omnipresent day-hot dirt. They were headed for a modest two-room cabin just a few minutes outside the town center where lived Elijah and the widowed Mrs. Anderson, built deliberate upwind of the main stable.

Bill tipped his gray, gold-tasseled hat — a war souvenir he seemed to never remove from his aging head — to the various folk about their various business in the ending hours of the day. He most often received a smile or a wave, or a return hat tip from the more stolid men, in response. Sheriff Hensley was a good man, most figured, and he was well liked.

Elijah did his own smiling and waving and hat tipping, except when he saw fourteen-year-old Molly Taggart sittin' on the porch of the boarding house and he felt in his stomach like there was a train engine headin' right for him. He made some noise like a dumbstruck giggle and turned away towards Bill so's she wouldn't see him blushing with humiliation.

Once they'd rode a few more minutes and Elijah got composed, he put Bill a question. "Ye ever feel like a coward?"

"Don't reckon so," Bill answered.

"Ye never get afraid?" Elijah asked, surprised but hopeful for some wisdom that would change him.

Bill chuckled. "Now I didn't say that, son."

"Watch'yer mean then by it?" 'Lijah said.

"A coward's a man what runs away from what he knows he has to do," Bill said. "A man's a real man and fulla courage when he does what he has to, even when he's afraid. 'Specially then."

Elijah screwed his face up a little, hard thinkin'. "So ye do get to feelin' afraid?" He asked.

"Every day, son," Bill said. "Every day, some ways. A man lookin' to better hisself looks to do somethin' that scares 'im every day, whether big or small."

'Lijah didn't quite understand it, but he knew he'd just heard something real important somehow. So without really knowing how he did it, he buried it away in that secret part of his young heart where was watered the seeds of knowledge that would, with care and time, grow up to a strong oak of manhood.

The Anderson home was wood with a tar-patched shingle roof and a stove pipe rising up from the kitchen side. Smoke plumed from it and signaled there'd be dinner waitin'. Ma would ask the Sheriff to stay and he'd decline with his customary "Thank ye, kindly, ma'am". And this is in fact how it went, when the man and the boy arrived to a warm but nervous – 'count of the prisoner – greeting from Elijah's Mama.

"Ye sure ye won't stay, Sheriff?"

"'Fraid I gotta be gettin' back to the office, find me some time to dress this doe, check up on my guest, as 'twere."

"Ye know, Sheriff, I don't rightly care for little 'Lijah troublin' ye at the office with that Briggs feller locked up in there," Ma said.

"I ain't little!" Elijah interjected.

"Settle yerself," Mama said. "Yer my little boy still, no matterin' how quick yer fixin' to grow up."

'Lijah harrumphed in a way which he immediately reckoned made him sound just like the little boy he was 'cused of bein', rather than the man he couldn't wait to be.

"Nothin' to be worryin' over s'far as Colter Briggs, ma'am," Bill said. "He's locked up real good waitin' the U.S. Marshals pickin' him up."

"Ain't that I don't trust ye, Sheriff, understand," Mama said. "Reckon most every folks in Cedar Bend here trust ye a dern sight. I only reckon it ain't a place for a little boy to be frequentin' as 'Lijah is doin' that jailhouse nigh daily. I heard tell that Briggs is a mean man, a right bad one what's was ridin' with the outlaw Holler Wade and robbin' Wells Fargo 'spresses up Utah Territory."

"Ye heard right, ma'am," Bill said. "But it ain't still any thing ye ought worry 'bout. Reckon 'im'll stay right put 'til them Marshals come in any day now."

"Well, all the better, but still I worry 'bout 'im scaring the boy, rough char'cter he is."

'Lijah started to protest but BIll held a hand up to stop him and spoke his piece on the matter. "Reckon, ma'am," Bill said. "And a'course it's yer decision in the matter, but I reckon that a boy itchin' to grow up to a man oughtta be doin' some things what scare 'im a little. 'Specially 'cause 't'ain't no real danger, all told."

Mama looked doubtful, brow all furrowed and lips apart like she was fixin' to say somethin', but she stopped herself and tried to say just a polite and a bit cold, but sincere, goodnight.

"Well, Sheriff..."

"Please, ma'am, 'Bill'."

Mama smiled then, despite herself, and then tried to disappear it real quick.

"Well, Bill, I thank ye again for takin' my boy out for a hunt and overall lookin' after him. A boy needs a man 'round. And I'll think over what ye said as regards him helpin' out round the office."

Bill smiled, removed the hat he never removed, and bowed a small bow, and said goodnight.

"Goodnight, Sheriff Hensley," Mama said. "Come on in, Elijah. Wash up and supper's awaitin'."

Bill's grin turned a mite sad and he wheeled 'round and swung himself up on the big roan and went his way into the evening.

***

The sun came up next day the way it always did and found Elijah gettin' hisself ready to do as he always did and mosey on up the way to the Sheriff's Office. He was 'spectin' Mama to give him a right hard time or maybe as prevent him from going up there and yet after he wolfed down the bowl of oats and milk what's always gave him strength for the day, she said nothin' but "I love ye, 'Lijah" and planted a motherly peck upon his brow. Seemed she was signing off on his continuin' education in law enforcement and general teachin' in growing up to a man and let him leave with a smile and a wave.

Elijah's stroll was a leisurely one, kicking up clouds of dirt for the hell of it, and taking in the sights and sounds that was nothin' pretty – the same stale frying grease and horse leavings and mud – but was beautifully home.

From a little ways, where she couldn't see him yet, 'Lijah spied Molly's brown curls and those eyes he couldn't make out from a distance but which he knew were an endless ocean of jade green. His stomach made a move to revolt against him, but he willed strong with his mind to shut it up and resolved to face one of those little fears which Bill was yammerin' on about yesterday.

Then he knew she saw him but she didn't 's'yet make it known and sat just looking out yonder. Then she turned her pretty face towards him and didn't do nothing else. 'Lijah dug down deep and felt something well up in him like a fire and tried to hide the shake of his hand as he touched it to the brim of his hat and then tipped it Molly's way and smiled. Like the blazing sun coming up, her smile beamed his way in reply and she waved.

Elijah felt somethin' he reckoned was a damn sight like what it felt like to win a grand battle or break a wild mustang, and he beamed back. Darn it all if Bill weren't right about facin' fears and betterin' a man's self. 'Lijah woulda swore he was eleven feet tall then. He seemed to ride a cloud the rest of the way to the Sheriff's Office.

Inside, Elijah found Old Man Holly reading a tattered wanted poster and muttering to himself something about honor and his youth. Nobody 'round town was quite sure if "Holly" was a Christian name or a family name for the man, but he was Bill's charity case, a war veteran and before that some's sort of merchant sailor, now missin' a right arm and always missin' and pinin' for better days that had come before. Playin' at guard and custodian was his stock in trade now, and everyone was always a-wonderin' and nearly marveling at the trust Sheriff Bill placed in the man, sour and ornery and often drunk as he was. But that was Bill's character and belief that if you gave people something for's to be responsible with they time enough lived up to what you was 'scpectin' of them. Hell, it seemed to be working with Elijah hisself, and 'Lijah found in the midst of this ponderin' a steady increasin' in his awe and respect for the lawman.

Holly looked up and grumbled something like a good morning to Elijah.

"Good morning," Elijah replied. "Where's Bill?"

"Ain't for knowin'."

There was a silence and a fly buzzed around somewhere's unseen.

"Pay ye a nickel tuh swab the deck here," Holly growled, using his strange sailor words in trying to get Elijah to mop up the floors.

"I'll do it for a look at our guest of honor," Elijah answered, in a daring mood.

Holly laughed and said, "Briggs? Why in tarnation... Don't right think Bill or yer Ma... eh, hell, what am I for carin'? Come on, then."

Holly led him into the back room which housed two cells with three iron-bar walls, the fourth wall being the back of the office and made of wood with iron-grated high windows. In the cell next to the one reserved for mostly over-rowdy cow punchers and other general minor miscreants to sleep off a little too much whiskey, Elijah looked into the blankly-staring, dirty, wickedly grinning rot-toothed face of Colter Briggs, bank robber, 's'posed murderer, and ridin' companion of the infamous outlaw Holler Wade.

"Howdy, pard'ner," Briggs snarled at 'Lijah.

"Pipe down," Holly barked back. He turned to Elijah. "Seen enough, boy?"

Elijah shook his head and looked and studied the man as he would any other animal. He took a cautious step forward, then another, and met the cruel gaze of the caged beast. "Why d'ye do what you do?" Elijah asked Briggs, playin' innocent with his tone of voice.

Briggs cackled and bared his blackened nub teeth. Suddenly, 'Lijah felt his heart creeping into his throat, fixin' to choke him, and his palms grew wet.

"Iff'n ye don't understand, boy," Briggs said, mystical. "Ye prolly never will."

"Ye 'fraid of hell?" 'Lijah croaked out.

Briggs about howled. "Not me, boy. Reckon there's the best dice and women and firewater a man could have."

"Ye never get no conscience 'bout hurtin' people, good honest folk?"

Briggs just spat at them and 'Lijah barely dodged the spittle and Holly caught some on his good arm, prolly thankin' God it was sleeved.

"Enough outta ye there!" Holly shouted and grabbed a tin cup off a table and slung it at the outlaw. It bounced off the grates with a clang and Briggs cackled like a lunatic and Holly took Elijah hard by the arm and yanked him out of the room, slamming the door behind him. The muted mad laughter continued other side of the door.

"Go on home, boy," Holly said, sweatin' likely the notion of word gettin' to Bill he'd let the boy see the prisoner.

'Lijah ran back to Ma's house, right scared out of his boots and feelin' mighty a coward and a fool for it.

***

Elijah slept past the sun next day and Ma 'ventually woke him and asked if he'd be going in town to help Sheriff Hensley and 'Lijah only grunted and pulled his hat over his eyes.

"Well, if ye ain't goin' in town, I've almighty 'mount of work for you to do 'round here," Ma said.

'Lijah groaned but, not wantin' to confess he was afraid and ashamed to go back to the jailhouse, submitted to the yoke of the broom and wash tub.

Hours passed in boring labor and his fingers was hurtin' from the washboard and his heart was pounding mysterious in his chest until he realized that he was still scared out of his wits 'bout that outlaw Briggs. He got real disgusted with hisself bein' a coward and all, what with Briggs bein' caged and not a danger to anyone 'cept in the way ghosts might be, which was to say it was all up in yer head.

He of a sudden had enough with all that and as the sun was beginning to go down resolved to head to Bill's on the double.

As he was coming up to the door of the Office, Bill was rushing out and heading for the post where he hitched his Roan. The sky was near full dark now.

"Where ye goin' all in a bustle?" Elijah said.

Bill passed him and tousled his hair and called over his shoulder: "Probably nothin', son, but heard tell Wade and company was out ridin' east of Cedar here."

"And yer goin alone?" The worry was a solid substance in Elijah's voice.

"Nothin' to be concerned about. Go check on Holly would ya? He's been a bit hard on the bottle I'm thinkin'."

'Lijah stood froze and guessed he was turnin' white.

"You'll be 'right, son. I trust ye."

That little sayin' was like courage that Elijah took by injection. By all rights Bill was puttin' him in charge and he felt mighty big and proud.

Inside, 'Lijah found Holly a sight worse than Bill had said, snoring something wild and drooling on his shirt, bottle balanced on his limp left hand, 'bout to fall and more'n half empty. 'Lijah felt something like pity for the fella but reckoned it weren't no excuse to shirk a man's duty.

All the same, Elijah set down and got to thinkin'. It seemed a lot had happened and he was reasonin' through it and mostly wonderin' why he was so afraid to begin with. Briggs was well enough secure that Bill seemed to not think twice about leaving him in the hands of a sleeping drunk and a young boy.

Some time passed in daydreamin', 'Lijah weren't sure how long but a good spell.

Suddenly, there was a loud clang behind the door to the cells. Another clang. 'Lijah's heart was immediate thundering like a galloping mustang and, somethin' almighty worse than his first meeting with Briggs was fixin' to choke him. Some chattering could be heard, muted as it was through the door. Elijah had to check. As if his hands and feet were not his own, he felt moved by some spirit to the door and shoved it open with a force what's surprised him. There, against the wall, was Briggs reaching up to the iron grating high up on the wood wall where was fixed two metal hooks, yanking away at the bars. Briggs turned at the sound of 'Lijah barging in and grinned his black grin and cackled and shouted, "Hurry up, now, boys!"

Elijah stood dumb and mute. His heart pounded in his head and ears and there was a ringing noise in his mind. He couldn't move. They was making a jailbreak right in front of his eyes.

CRAAACK!

The boards came down back out into the alley and Elijah spied three men on horseback, two of them with rope tied to the hooks and their horses speeding away some yards as the pent up tension from the pullin' on the grate was released. They was howlin' and hootin' like some nightmare creatures what's a witch had crossed 'tween and Injun and a rabid dog.

Briggs nodded and black-grinned at the boy and darted out into the dirt road.

What was 'Lijah going to do? Panic gripped him with icy ghost fingers at his throat. He couldn't let the outlaw just walk out of town... Bill had trusted him... but what could a little boy do?

Crack. Clack-clack. Crack. Clack-clack. Crack. Clack-clack.

A few flashes, along with the sound of shots, and the two riders that was pulling ropes toppled off their mounts to the dust, as the ponies fled for the hills.

Bill with his Winchester. 'Lijah couldn't see him off to the left somewhere but the evidence was sure.

The remaining horseman reared his mustang up on hind legs, dashed a quick circle to make a hard target, and drew two pistols as he did.

'Lijah looked back with time enough to see Holly, shaken from his sleep by the ruckus, darting out the front door of the office. Coward!

Crack. Clack-clack. Crack. Clack-clack.

The second shot caught the last rider in the arm and he fumbled with the reins and his horse neighed fierce and ran another circle.

'Lijah's hands were slick with sweat but he felt then that he could move them and some kind of lightning shot through his body. He turned back into the outer office as he saw Briggs scrambling to nab a pistol off one of the dead men outside the wall.

In the office he yanked open the drawer of the desk where Holly had been sleeping, hoping for a miracle and finding one in the form of a .36 Navy, the old drunk's service pistol. He broke the cylinder out. Loaded. He jammed it back in and ran back to the cell bars.

Briggs was back inside with his back turned, taking cover behind the shattered wall and firing off to the left, trying to hit Bill, who 'Lijah still couldn't see.

Crack. Clack-clack from the left. Clicks and bangs and flying fire from the surviving rider.

Bill rode into view. Cracks and bangs and they were hit at the same time: Bill in the arm, his Winchester falling to the dirt and the body of the last rider joining it some yards to the right. "Bill!" Elijah shouted, as Briggs was training his pistol on the unarmed Sheriff.

Briggs jolted at the call, turned without seemin' to think, and cackled as he spotted the boy.

'Lijah cocked the revolver. Click-click.

"Ye wouldn't dare, yuh yella, lilly livered sonofab—"

The prisoner's taunt was cut short by a sharp boom and a leap of muzzle flame. Red plumed on his dirty shirt and he gasped in shock.

"Wha..." was the last thing Briggs muttered as 'Lijah fanned the hammer and another boom made a fresh red flower on the outlaw's shirt. He sagged down to his knees and fell forward, eyes glassy and not believin' what'd happened to him.

There was a mad yell and Elijah figgered after a minute of his head clearin' that it was his own voice yellin' and there was a tear in his eye and his pulse was racin'.

Bill was gone.

What'd happened? Was he alive? The outlaw bodies laid all about and it was eery dead still.

"Bill?!" Elijah called into the sudden silence. There was a gentle weight on Elijah's shoulder. He turned 'round and looked up into the strong, kind eyes of the Sheriff. Bill winced and tried to make it look like a smile. With his good arm he tousled Elijah's hair once more.

"Yer shot!" Elijah said.

Bill brushed at the air like he didn't care none at all and said, "Take a lot more than Holler Wade and gaggle-a dunces to take out Ol' Sheriff Hensely."

Elijah smiled and hugged him without thinkin' twice. "I'm sorry, son," Bill said.

"What for?"

"For leavin' ye here. And for trustin' Holly to be brave. Ye coulda been killed. I shoulda known it was a trick they was playin', that news about them ridin' out east. Tell the truth I didn't think that band would care 'nough to try 'n' break Briggs."

"Nah, I should be the sorry one," Elijah said.

Bill looked shocked and his eyebrows 'bout went through the roof. "What in hell for?" Bill near shouted. "And pardon my cussin'."

"I just sat here froze and scared and they might've killed ye if I hadn't come to of a sudden."

"But ye did, son. And what did I tell ye 'bout what a man does, one fulla courage?"

"That he does what he has to, even when he's scared."

"'Specially then," Bill finished.

"But I din't feel no courage in it."

"But ye did it anyhow, even afraid."

Elijah shrugged, feelin' guilty and not knowing' why.

"I killed a man," Elijah almost sobbed.

"I told ye there was a season for that and ye asked me how a body was for knowin' that season. Ye know what makes a man have courage, and do what he has to do even if it's killin'?"

Elijah shook his head.

"Love."

Elijah jolted up and said with confusion. "Where's there love in shootin' a man to death?"

"For a boy who knows so almighty much about the Good Book, you'd think him for knowin' that."

"I don't understand."

"The Good Lord Hisself said, 'Greater love hath no man than this, that he may lay down his life for his friends.'"

Elijah gazed with some hidden understanding into those kind eyes.

"And I thank that same Lord ye didn't lay down that life of yers, but you was damn well ready to give it for me. And that's what we was called to do in war. What yer Pa did too. And what any of us soldiers would do a thousand times again for the folk we love. And I say that makes you lovin'. And that makes you fulla courage. And… that makes you a man, son."

Elijah felt like he might cry but he shoved it down and end of it said nothing.

"Now, come on. Let's get you back to yer Ma," Bill said and wrapped his good arm around Elijah's shoulder and walked him out into the night.

And as they walked side by side, man and man, Elijah felt so tall he almost ducked to keep from scrapin' the top of his head on the moon.

Just in Time for Nothing

GAIUS WARNER

"Guess I had to travel ten thousand miles just to sweep the floor."

His father did not look up. Lee scraped the stiff bristles along the wood floor a few more times, then continued.

"I ought to be grateful, really. Other boys can sweep up any time they please, but I suppose I was born unto difficulty."

The man at the counter answered, but slowly, "Lee, I'm trying to keep count, if you please."

Lee hushed up. He swept as loud as he could, but that was just as ineffective as his complaining. He finished the room, then opened the door to get rid of the dust.

Outside was a bustling little town by the name of Redrock. The dirt road was wide enough to accommodate horses, wagons, and plenty of pedestrians. Most walkers stayed to the wooden sidewalks, clomping up and down the streets. The men looked snappy in their dark suit jackets and hats, the ladies just as fine in their long dresses, white fabric shining in the hot sun. Laughter bounced off of every shop and house and eating establishment. The colors were vibrant and multifarious – greens, blues, shocking whites and gentle browns. Just past the edge of town could be seen the boundless frontier, sticker bushes carpeting the ground.

Lee sighed yet again and shook his broom out from under the awning that shaded the front of his father's store. He wiped his hands on his apron and went back inside. His father was folding up papers and collecting his effects. Pulling on a jacket, he addressed Lee.

"Mind the shop for a while. I won't be long."

Lee leaned the broom in its place and resisted the urge to sigh again.

"Yes sir."

"Just going to the bank." He picked up his things and stepped to the door. "If anybody asks for credit, tell them you're not permitted to extend it without me here."

"I know that already."

Mr. Taylor looked at his son over his spectacles.

"Yes sir," Lee corrected himself.

He left with a nod, the door shutting out the noise of the street. Lee leaned on the counter.

Plenty of apothecaries in St. Louis, his father had said, but folks out in the territory would be glad to have him. That's why Job Taylor had struck out West in the first place. Lee remembered waving him off, his mother holding his hand tight. As tight as he'd held hers the day she finally slipped away into that sweet by and by. It wasn't long after her death that a letter arrived to set Mr. Taylor's affairs in order. First and foremost, arranging for his only child to join him in Arizona.

Lee's grief had faded along with the eastern horizon as the steam machine rumbled its way ever west, west, west! Throwing himself into his father's arms on the platform, he'd been too exhilarated even to cry. Mr. Taylor had cried.

At first sight, Redrock was everything he could have hoped for. As he walked alongside his father down the street for the first time, he half-expected to see bandits shooting it out in the local saloon. It was upon pointing out that particular establishment that he had his first disappointment.

"That's no place for an upright young man like you," his father said, sternly.

And that was just the beginning. Turned out, Redrock wasn't even as wild as St. Louis. No desperadoes galloping furiously through the streets, no casual revolvers fired off at all hours, and not one prospector riding into town to crow over newfound gold. What kind of frontier town was this, anyway?

He asked his father about it, but Mr. Taylor only shook his head. "Afraid you're a little late for all that."

A little late. A little late for jingling spurs and rearing horses and the crack of a rifle defending the wagons. Plenty of time for sweeping the floor though. And minding the shop and learning to measure herbs and shine his shoes. Just in time for that. Just in time for nothing.

The door to the apothecary opened, letting in the hubbub from outside. Lee looked and then stood up quickly. Striding into his father's store were two Indians. Tall, with long hair, and sober expressions that could only be called menacing. They seemed surprised to see him. They muttered one to another, then one of them spoke. He had a dark brown hat with a band.

It sounded inquisitive, but Lee couldn't make out a word of it. Whatever the question was, the brown-hatted Indian asked it again, stepping closer. His partner, whose own hat hung by a cord around his neck, revealing streaks of grey in his long hair, stepped to the far corner – taking position, it seemed to Lee.

"I – I'm sorry?" he said, finally. "I'm not supposed to...to extend credit without my father here. He's at the bank."

Brown Hat turned to his companion. He was obviously frustrated. Grey Hair said a few unintelligible words, then chuckled. Brown Hat clicked his tongue and turned back to Lee. He was agitated now.

But the young man was no more able to understand his jabberings than before. Lee didn't know what to do. He didn't know anything about Indians beyond what he'd read and seen in the shows. And that sure wasn't pretty. All he could do was apologize again.

The tall Indian shook his head and stepped back from the counter. Grey Hair didn't seem bothered, but Brown Hat spoke rapidly. Lee felt sweat starting to run down his back. He thought of the scattergun in the stock room.

As if the man had read his mind, the Indian with the brown hat stomped past the counter and turned right, leaning into the back room. Lee froze as the man shouted once, then twice into the back. Lee was shaken out of his stupor by the shouting.

"Hey! Hey you, mister!" he called, stepping up behind Brown Hat. "You can't go back there."

He put a hand on the Indian's arm, who immediately jerked it back and rounded on him. He spoke more in his strange tongue, and Lee wondered if he ought to call for help. But Grey Hair stepped closer and calmed his companion. He spoke softly – conspiratorially? – and gestured toward the door. Brown Hat was fit to be tied, but something Grey Hair whispered made him smile. Lee disliked the smile more than he did the yelling. The loud one tipped his brown hat and spoke once more to Lee. Whatever he said provoked raucous laughter from Grey Hair, and the two moved quickly out of the shop, slamming the door behind them.

In his mind Lee plotted his course of action. He would check their position from the window, then bar the door. No, better bar the door first, couldn't be too careful. After ascertaining their location, he would dash to the stock room and fetch the scattergun. Was it loaded? Surely Dad wouldn't keep it unloaded. But what if it was? Did he know how to load it? He'd seen it done, but – know what, he wouldn't worry about it. He'd get the gun and take a defensive position in the doorway to the stockroom. Just the sight of it ought to be enough to scare them off. That way if they came in the back, he could cover that door too. But what if they surrounded him and came in both entrances? Should he go upstairs? That would leave them free to ransack the store, but Dad – The front door opened again. Lee started and whirled around. He hadn't moved an inch since the two men had left. Now they were back, and he was a sitting duck!

But it was just his father, papers in hand. "I'm home," he announced, closing the door. "Sorry about the delay, bit of a stir going on outside. You alright?"

Lee uprooted himself and ran to his father. Mr. Taylor was stunned at first, then embraced his son, quietly asking what was the matter. The instant he felt sufficiently comforted, the boy broke loose and grabbed his father by the forearms.

"Dad, some people came in while you were gone." He took a deep breath. "Indians, Dad. Two of 'em."

There was a long pause. Lee tried to steady himself, unsure how volatile a reaction to expect. But after a beat or two he felt the need to reemphasize the situation.

"In the store. Two Indians."

"They want credit, or...?"

"Did they want – I don't know what they wanted, Dad. I couldn't understand a word of it!"

"Alright, just calm down now."

"I am calm!" Lee shouted. "They came in here, talking about God-knows-what, and getting in my face and laughing at me. One of them tried to force his way into the back, hollering something fierce!"

"Into the back? What are you talking about?"

"I barely managed to hold him back! I mean, I didn't *hold* him back so much, his buddy pulled him away."

"His buddy pulled him." Mr. Taylor took off his glasses and rubbed his eyes with two fingers. "Son, you sure these weren't just customers?"

"They were Indians, Dad!"

"We get all sorts in this town, Lee. There's bound to be Indians once in a while."

Lee groaned and tried hard not to stamp his foot like a child. "Dad, you're not listening to me!"

"I am listening. I'm sorry you were scared, but there's going to be tough folks coming in here sometimes. You're going to have to learn how to handle that." He moved to the counter, dropping off his papers. "Alright?"

"Alright, but can I just ask you one question?" His father nodded. "Is that scattergun in the back loaded?"

Mr. Taylor's eyes widened in shock, then he burst out laughing. Lee felt hot anger flush his face. He bit his tongue. He would not cry, not now.

"Aw Lee," he caught his breath. "Try not to shoot the paying customers, will you please?"

"They weren't customers, they were Indians."

"Now that's enough," Job Taylor snapped. "This conversation is over."

It was.

Lee was grateful for the chance to go fetch the day's mail. As he hitched up Sterling, he fumed. He felt ridiculous for the way he'd frozen in front of those men, but equally angry at his father for not believing him about the terror he'd faced. Climbing up onto the seat, he snapped a command at the aging horse and leaned forward, elbows on his knees.

He navigated the slow roads of Redrock to the station while envisioning his how his father might react to sight of his scalp nailed to the front door. That would show him. Should have taken him more seriously. Lee steered the wagon alongside the rail station and pulled on the reins. He tied old Sterling properly, although the horse was too obedient to run off anyhow.

The 2:40 had just departed. As Lee carried boxes from the storeroom to the wagon. he noticed the gathering crowd. They were familiar faces, laughing and kind, real Redrock men. But they were mounted, armed and packed up for a few days, if Lee was any judge. As he slid another box of powders across the splinters, he hollered to a mustached man he recognized. The man slowed and came over.

"Job Taylor's boy, ain't you?"

"Lee's my name. What's going on?"

"Roundup. Couple fellows tried to make off with about a hundred head yesterday, and now we got to get 'em back."

Lee darted his eyes across the men with a whole new respect.

"A roundup?" he asked. "Like a posse? You gonna bring the rustlers to justice?"

The large man laughed heartily. "Land sakes! No, son. Marshals already caught the rustlers. All's left is to catch the steers!"

Well, that was still something. The man was clucking to his horse and moving on.

"Wait!" he called. "Can I come?"

Another friendly laugh. "That'd be up to your Pap, young sir. But I think we got things well in hand." He waved without looking back. "Give him my best, will you please?"

Despite the slow traffic of Redrock, Lee did his best to hurry home with the wagon. He pulled up behind the shop, and his father came out to unload.

"Dad!" he called, dropping the reins and scrambling down. "Dad, there's a cattle roundup going out today. Rustlers tried to make off with the herd."

"Mmhmm," grunted Mr. Taylor, stepping up into the wagon bed. "Heard about that. Pack of fools. Trying to steal cows in a place like this."

Lee thought it best to be helpful just now. He took the boxes from his father and set them beside the door.

"Are you going with them?"

"Me?" laughed Mr. Taylor. "No, I've got plenty to keep me busy."

"I guess," said Lee, nonchalant as he dared, "You'd get to be a cowboy, though."

His father chuckled. "You're a good boy, Lee. You know that?" He handed him another box. "A real good boy."

Lee waited. Then couldn't stand it any longer. "Can I go?"

The answer came too quickly, "No. Too much needs doing around here."

"But why not?"

His father blinked slowly and slid the last box to the edge of the wagon. He hoisted it up and walked to the door. "Put Sterling away and come help me unpack."

Lee walked the horse to the stable. He was just putting him in his stall when he heard the commotion. Hoofbeats and shouts, laughter. It was the roundup setting out. He listened to the noise of their departure, his hand on Sterling's bridle. He stood there for a full minute. Then two. Then he smiled and patted Sterling's neck.

Not quite an hour later, he was urging the old warhorse to a gallop, just past the outskirts of Redrock. He needed to go fast. First to catch up with the other riders, and second – well, second to make sure no one saw him, least of all his father. He figured he could gain on the men before nightfall if he kept up a fast pace, then look for their camp in the dark. Sterling seemed to perk up at the chance to really run, so Lee gave him his head.

The plains opened up before him like milk and honey. The dense sticker bushes were patterned with brown patches of dirt and sand, a few stubborn trees making the climb above the surface. The sky was wide and open, and the high hills formed a benevolent boundary to the quiet wilderness. A roadrunner darted across his path. Lee felt a grin tug at his mouth and he let out a loud whoop, urging his horse on to greater speeds. The sun sank lower, giving a golden wash to all below, even the scrub casting long shadows for the young man to trample as he passed.

Long before he would have expected, Sterling started to slow, resisting his kicks and coaxes. His hoofs scraped the ground as he came to a walk, blowing long breaths in exhale.

"You lazy son of a gun," said Lee.

The sun vanished all at once and the stars came out. The horse kept moving, but not quickly. Behind him Lee could just barely see the glow of Redrock illuminating the night. He continued on the path before him, but his pulse began to quicken. He strained his eyes for firelight.

Just as he started to wonder if this had all been a bad idea, he spied an orange glow up ahead. It was off the path, but there was a way through the bushes. He dismounted to lead the horse. He rehearsed what he would say, hopeful they would all find it a grand thing and maybe sit him down at the fire, the man of the hour. He heard a horse snort nearby and made for the sound.

Only two mounts were tied up at the spot. He left Sterling there and walked toward the light. One man was bending over the fire. They must have left him to make camp while the rest finished up with the cows.

"Hello, partner!" he called out.

The man looked up. His hat was hanging by a string, and his long hair had familiar grey streaks. Lee stopped short. He turned to run, but his arms were caught by a strong grip behind him. It was Brown Hat, looking meaner than ever.

Lee shouted and twisted furiously to break loose, but the Indian wouldn't let go. He shouted in his infernal language. Lee panicked, thrashing and flailing, but Brown Hat pulled him close and pinned his arms. He called for help, but the man put a red hand firm over his mouth.

Over his head, the two campers spoke rapidly. Their voices were intense, even excited, to Lee's ears. The boy was carried and then dropped alongside the fire. Immediately he tried to spring up and run, but Brown Hat's hands squeezed tight on his shoulders, holding him down. Grey Hair came around and squatted, looking him directly in the eye. The shadows danced on his lined, serious face. The old Indian began to speak, but Lee was just as confused as ever. He repeated himself, slower. All Lee could do was shake his head.

"I'm sorry. I'm sorry, I don't know. Please, just let me go."

It came to Lee's mind that right about now his father would be stirring up supper.

His captors held an indecipherable conversation. Lee strained to understand, but there wasn't one word of English coming out of their mouths. Were they deciding whether to let him go? Or debating over death, slavery or ransom?

In time, the men seemed to come to a resolution. Grey Hair leaned close. He held up a hand before Lee's face. He grunted sharply, then emphasized the hand again. Lee nodded, but had no idea what he was agreeing to. Brown Hat released him. He started to rise, but a sound *slap* hit him across the ears, and he slumped to the ground. Grey Hair held up his hand again with severe eyes. Then came the first word he recognized out of the mouth of the Indian.

"No."

Lee inhaled quickly. He nodded and whispered.

"Okay."

Grey Hair stood to his feet and stalked off, muttering. Brown Hat came around and leaned close and spat a few more savage words his way. He held up a coil of rope and waved it in his face. Lee nodded.

"No sir. I won't run. Honest I won't."

Lee sat as still as he could. Grey Hair brought over a plate of stew, and despite whispered fears of poison, the boy was ravenous. In time, the fire burned down and the red men lit cigars. Every sensational story of precise tortures and primeval witchcraft he had ever heard filled his mind with remarkable clarity. He just tried to look small and scared. It wasn't hard.

Finally, Brown Hat flicked his cigar butt into the dying fire and stood to his feet. Grey Hair took a few deep drags to finish his as well. The younger man stalked back to his captive and stood over him. Lee looked up. A blanket was thrown in his face. By the time he pulled it off, Brown Hat had gone to his bed and was laying himself down. Grey Hair grunted to get his attention, and Lee looked. He held up a hand like before and repeated his single English word.

"No."

Lee nodded. Grey Hair gestured to the countryside in all directions and spoke more nonsense. He shook his head vigorously and repeated his monosyllable, this time as a question. Lee nodded again.

"Yes sir."

Grey Hair went to bed. The embers of the fire glowed beneath the charred black branches. Lee put his head down and pulled the blanket over himself. The Indians both snored before long, Brown Hat loud and raucous, Grey Hair with whistling exhalations. Lee was not tired. He was wound tight like a spring. How long should he wait? Just a little bit more, he told himself, hour after hour.

When the fire had gone cold, and starlight was the only illumination left, Lee made his move. Inch by agonizing inch, he slipped the blanket off. With anxious awareness of every grain of sand disturbed, carefully, carefully he stood to his feet. No movement from the Indians. He backed slowly away from the campsite, the chill of the night taking hold of his bones. Nothing moved. He turned and stalked off into the darkness.

He moved away from the road, not daring to go back for poor old Sterling. He chose his steps fearfully, silently, away from the camp, and down the slow incline. The terrain dropped off into a shallow gully, and he slid down, crouching at the bottom to listen. All he heard was a pack of coyotes screaming in the distance like desert demons.

He picked his way through the prickly undergrowth, cutting himself so often he stopped bothering about it. Sometimes he had to clamber up the sides a little to get around the rocks and other obstacles. All the time he moved toward Redrock. At least he hoped so. He couldn't see above the gully, and didn't dare stop for a peek. Away was as good as home at the moment.

In time, speed overcame his caution. He was too far away to wake up Grey Hair and Brown Hat. Of course, knowing Indians, they'd be silent, deadly killers, and he'd never see them coming. He stumbled and fell often, but he couldn't stop. All the time the thought of his worrying father pained his heart.

"Faster Lee," he whispered, "Faster!"

One by one, the stars winked out and the pastel dawn began. No sunrise yet, but he could tell the sticker bushes from the saguaros by sight now, not just shape. He was bone tired. His careful steps had become weary shuffles. One of those shuffles alarmed a coiled-up rattler. The mean snake was lurking beneath a big rock in a ring the size of Lee's hat, rattle waving hypnotically above its head. Lee leaped for the side of the gully and pulled himself up by roots and rocks, rolling over the top and gasping for breath.

The sun was shimmering on the skyline now. He rolled to his knees. There it was. There was Redrock. He could hear the sounds of the morning bustle drifting over the plain. Lee stood to his feet to thank his Maker when another sound came to his ears. Hoofbeats. Coming down the road, distant but gaining fast, were two men on horseback, with a third, familiar creature in tow.

Lee abandoned any semblance of strategy or good sense. Drawing on the strength that only fear can supply, he lit out for the town. He knew they would see him, he just had to hope they were too far to catch him. Or too smart to try it in broad daylight.

His lungs burned. A loud holler carried over the wind. Grey Hair was pointing at him and calling out in desperate tones, while Brown Hat urged his horse to a gallop. The wind of Lee's frantic pace whipped in his ears. He crossed into town, but his pursuers did not slow. He stumbled onto the wooden sidewalk, his boots banging on the wood as he coughed for air. He grabbed the door handle of his father's apothecary. It was unlocked. He threw the door open and fell inside.

"Lee!" came a shout.

It was his father. Lee scrambled to his feet and lurched past him, vaguely noticing two other men in the room. He grabbed the door-frame for support as he turned into the stock room.

"Lee, what are you doing?"

He grabbed the scattergun. He could only hope it was loaded. He turned around. His father had open shock on his face.

"Watch out Dad, they're coming!"

"What are you –"

The door banged open again. Brown Hat stood in the doorway, tall and severe. Lee gave a shout and tried to push past his father, but Job Taylor grabbed the barrel of the gun and pointed it upward. There was confusion and shouting and Lee's vision spotted and fuzzed. Next thing he knew, he was held tight again by the arms. Brown Hat and Grey Hair were in the shop now. And his father had taken the weapon.

The Indians began to speak, and the two others, whom Lee noticed had badges on their jackets, began to interrogate them. Lee's father turned to his son.

"Where have you been?"

"I went after the roundup, but they caught me, Dad! They grabbed me and hurt me and wouldn't let me leave. They were gonna kill me, I just know it. I snuck away."

At this, Mr. Taylor joined in the conversation, which was growing louder by the minute. Lee was surprised. He never knew his father spoke Indian. The man with the badge suggested that Lee remove himself from the room, and Mr. Taylor sent him upstairs. Lee was only too glad to get away, and collapsed onto his bed.

He didn't realize he had fallen asleep until he noticed his father shaking his shoulder.

"Come on downstairs, now."

Back in the front room, the only ones remaining were his father and the two Indians. Lee shrank back, but his father gently guided him forward. Grey Hair was smiling. Brown Hat still looked annoyed.

"Lee, I'd like you to meet Domingo de la Torre, and his son Fortunato."

Grey Hair inclined his head. Brown Hat just laughed at what must have been the look on Lee's face. He spoke to Mr. Taylor, who also chuckled politely. Lee looked up, curious. His father put a hand on his shoulder.

"It's Spanish, son. They're Pima, from south of the border. Good people. Good customers."

Lee felt weak. "No. Dad, you don't understand, they – they *hurt* me!"

"I never said they weren't rough, but they're not bad men. They were going to bring you back this morning. Not their fault you can't speak their language."

The boy felt the whole episode transfigure before his eyes. He supposed from one perspective he had been something of an inconvenience to the two men. But he wasn't about to apologize. That would be just too humiliating. He settled for quick eye contact and then lowered his gaze.

As the men made their farewells, Lee stood quiet. Maybe if he prayed hard enough, God would let him fall through the floorboards so this whole story could end. But the man with the brown hat – Mr. de la Torre, he supposed – called his name. He had a wide grin on his face. Lee figured he deserved the mockery. But while he couldn't understand what the man said to him, the extended hand was unmistakable. He hesitated, checked with his father, and shook the Indian's hand. The older de la Torre smiled at him and put a hand on his shoulder. They nodded to Mr. Taylor, opened the door and left.

Lee said nothing. He could only imagine the punishment headed his way after this. At least they had brought Sterling back. He waited for his father to speak.

"Lee. Why don't you come with me?"

It was like he was seeing Redrock for the first time, familiar details standing out in a way he'd never noticed before. Together they crossed the busy street to the last place he could have expected. His father pushed open the swinging doors and gestured for Lee to enter the saloon.

The place was empty that early in the morning, but his father took a table and ordered from the friendly bartender. He laid his broom aside and brought a small glass with whiskey for Mr. Taylor, and a taller glass of milk for Lee. The boy didn't know what to think. His father folded his hands and they locked eyes.

"I was worried about you last night."

"I know Dad. I'm sorry."

"Had half the town out looking for you. Figured we'd come after you in the morning if you didn't turn up. Lucky those fellows found you."

"I guess so," said Lee.

A short pause.

"Did you really sneak back through the desert in the middle of the night by yourself?"

"Yes sir."

Lee knew he was in for it now. Here came the thunder. But his father only lifted his glass and held it. Lee's eyes widened, but his father's mouth twitched in a tiny smile. He lifted his cup high and Mr. Taylor clinked them together.

"Drink up, then, wild man."

His skin and clothes were covered in dried blood and dirt. His bones ached and his head was throbbing. He was exhausted. But somewhere deep down, in his heart maybe, something warm and golden was shining.

"I miss your mother," said Mr. Taylor. He sighed and looked out the window at the little wooden town. "She would have loved it here."

They sat in silence for a few more minutes. Lee felt like he ought to say something, but it felt right to be still and quiet, just the two of them. In time, Mr. Taylor took a deep breath.

"Well sir. Should we get back to it?"

Lee nodded. "Okay."

They scraped their chairs on the wooden floor. His father paid the man and thanked him. Just before they left the darkened room, though, Lee spoke up.

"Dad?"

Mr. Taylor turned to look.

"I love it here too."

His father smiled and clapped his son on the back. He opened the door and the two men stepped out to join the clamor of the town.

THE END

A Notched Gun

WALT COBURN

Sam Graybull was a killer. He proved it now as he backed slowly out of the Valley Bank with a smoking Colt in one hand and a gunnysack full of currency in the other. The teller had made a move for the automatic below the money counter. Sam Graybull's bullet had caught the unfortunate man between the eyes.

The cashier, his movements sluggish from stark fear, made a break for the side door and was shot in the back.

"You'll be next," he told the young lady stenographer, "if you let out one yap."

The blizzard outside muffled the sound of the shots. There was no one abroad in the little storm-swept cow town to block San Graybull's departure. He mounted the horse that stood humped in the snow. In five minutes he was lost in the storm, made thicker by the shadows of dusk. He left no telltale sign. Because the country between Milk River and the Bad Lands was as familiar as a child's back yard, he had no fear of capture. He tied the sackful of money to his saddle and fashioned a cigaret with thick, blunt fingers that were steady.

"That damn' bank dude's mouth flopped open shore comical." The rattle of Sam Graybull's laugh was blurred by the wind.

No fear of pursuit marred the killer's flight. He knew the ways of sheriff's posses. They would hole up at the first ranch. That is why he had held off till the storm broke, then rode into town and stuck up the bank. A one man job. Cunningly planned, cold bloodedly executed. The lives he had taken were but tally notches on his gun, no more. He would boast about it when he got drunk.

"That other'n piled up like a beef."

The storm swirled and moaned. The horse drifted with the wind, headed south for the Bad Lands. A man could hole up there and get plenty drunk. Grub in the cabin. Wood enough for a month. Hay a-plenty. A keg of moonshine licker. When a man got hard up for company, there was Pete Peralta and his wife across the river. Pete was a damn' fool but he knowed how to keep his mouth shut. Pete was all right. Just didn't have the guts to go out and take chances, that was all. Mebbe if it wasn't fer the missus, Pete might swap a hayfork fer a gun and pick up some easy money. Pete's missus was just a young thing. Purty enough, so far as looks went. Kinda quiet. Scairt, like as not, because she wa'n't used to men that had guts. But she had sense. Close mouthed like most 'breed women. No damn' sheriff'd ever git anything outa Rose Peralta.

It was getting dark now. Black as a hat. Sam Graybull shrank into his buffalo coat and let his horse drift along. He rode good horses. Whenever Sam Graybull stole a horse he picked a good one. It was nearly a hundred miles into the Larb Hills where they dropped in timbered ridges to meet the Missouri River. To travel all night in a blizzard was only part of a man's job. The same as killing those two bank dudes. And by evening tomorrow he would be at his cabin in the Bad Lands.

"That keg'll look good."

Sam Graybull liked whisky. He liked whisky like most men like women. Liked the color of it in a glass. Liked the gurgle of the stuff as it spilled out of a jug into a tin cup. Talk about music. The burn of it when a man tilted a jug and drank it thataway. God, fer a drink right now.

But Sam Graybull dared not drink till he got home. Tried it onct. Fell off a horse and froze both feet sleepin' in the snow. Peter Peralta was horse huntin' and found him. Pete's missus taken care of him. Pete wasn't much of a hand to drink. A few shots and Pete had a-plenty.

Just enough to make that fiddle talk good. "The Red River Jig" and "Hell Among the Yearling's" and "Cross Eyed Moses." 'Breed tunes.

Sam hadn't seen Pete and his missus since early last spring. They were the only friends he claimed. A man on the dodge can't have many friends. Not when there's a big bounty on his scalp. That's the way most of the boys got theirs. Trustin' somebody. Hell, them fool posses never got nowhere. Milled around. And when they followed Sam Graybull they kept bunched. Damn' right they did.

Sam had been in Wyoming all summer. Gamblin' some amongst the sheep shearers. Gettin' drunk and eatin' good. Nobody the wiser. Who'd look around sheep camps fer a cow hand? Then he'd up and shot that Mexican shearer and had to drift back into Montana again. Too quick on the trigger.

Sam's rattling laugh broke forth again. He took out his .45 and with the nail file blade of his jacknife, he made two fresh notches on the gun's bone handle. That was the Indian in him. Sam was about a quarter breed Sioux. He was proud of those notches. Six, all told, counting the two bank dudes. Not bad fer a man thirty-one. He'd tell Pete and his missus. Pete'd grin kinda silly. The missus'd just sit and shiver like she was took with a chill. Scairt of a man that had guts. A man that was quick on the trigger.

Into the black maw of the cañons and draws. Snow piling in till a man felt smothered. Black as a hat. Cold. Give a dollar fer a drink. Hell, give five dollars. Ten. There was money a-plenty in that sack. Whisky money.

Topping out on a long ridge. Into a dawn that was the color of dirty slate. A wind that bit plumb into a man's innards. Didn't dast drop into a ranch or even a sheep camp fer grub. There'd be no fool sign fer a posse to pick up. Nobody but Pete knew of that little log cabin tucked away in a pocket of the Bad Lands. Pines and brush and rocks. Grub cached. Shoot a black-tail buck or a yearlin'. What's two days without grub? Make a man eat good when he got it. Whisky and meat. Good whisky and fat meat. Half way home now. Safe as dog in a hole.

Keep to the coulees, just under the rim of the ridges. No use skylin-in' a man's self. All day. Horse gittin' laig weary. Stumbled into a badger hole. No harm done. Wind that shriveled a man's heart. Wind that cut the hide on a man's face. Feet like ice cakes. Like the blood was dried up. God, but that whisky'd send it chargin' through a man's veins, though. Fill a jug and go acrost to Pete Peralta's. A man needed talk when he'd bin alone so long. Pete'd drag out the fiddle. "Red River Jig." "Hell among the Yearlin's." "Blue Bottles."

He pulled into his hidden cañon that afternoon. A frost seared, fur clad figure, red eyed from the wind and loss of sleep. A lone figure in a vast white world. Cold, hungry, craving whisky as a man on a parched desert craves water. With a fortune tied in a gunnysack. Two fresh notches on the bone handle of a short barreled Colt .45. A laugh rattling in his throat.

Hay in the barn. Pete had put up that hay. The spring above the cabin was warm. It never froze. Had an iron taste to it.

Sam Graybull watered and fed his gaunt horse. While no law of God or man had weight with the killer, he never violated that creed of the range that commands its men to care for a horse that has carried a man. After that he may look to his own comfort.

Sam Graybull found the whisky keg buried under the hay. He found a tin cup, and with a corner of his fur coat he wiped some of the dust from inside it. Then he squatted there by the keg and drank a cup of whisky as if the stuff were water. He sat there for better than half an hour. Drinking until the ache thawed from his bones and the hunger pains left his empty stomach. Now and then he laughed. The horse would give a start and look around, ears erect. Sam Graybull's laugh was unlike the laughter of any other man because there was no humor in it. More like a death rattle.

He was steady enough on his feet when he got up and went to the cabin. As steady as a man can be when he has been frozen into the saddle for a night and a day, and when he is bundled in fur coat and chaps and four buckle overshoes.

"Fill a jug and go visit Pete Peralta. To hell with cookin'. Pete's missus'll sling up some grub." His cracked, frost blackened lips split in a grin as he saw smoke coming from the Peralta cabin, across the river among the skeleton cottonwoods.

He found a jug and filled it. Then he kicked off his chaps and located a pair of snowshoes. It was as easy goin' afoot as it was a-horseback. He slung the jug about his shoulder with a bit of rope. Then he took his carbine and fitted it into a worn buckskin sheath.

"Whisky. Ca'tridges. All set." Then he remembered the money in the gunnysack. "Whisky's takin' holt." He hid the money in the hay. Then, shuffling along on his webs, he crossed the river to Pete Peralta's place.

II

Even before he rapped on the door, Sam Graybull sensed that something was wrong at the home of Pete Peralta. Horses in the hay corral, nibbling from the snow capped stack. Gate down. No tracks around. Cattle, gaunt flanked and hollow eyed, bawling for water in the lower pasture. Woodpile buried in the snow. Yet there was smoke coming from the chimney. A light inside, against the coming dusk.

"Come in!" Was that the voice of Pete Peralta? Sam could not see through the window. Frost had made the panes opaque.

Cautiously Sam Graybull opened the door. His jug and carbine laid aside, he held his Colt in his hand, the hammer thumbed back. He kicked the door open.

For a moment Sam Graybull stood there, half crouched, ready. Then he straightened. The gun hammer lowered gently and the weapon went back into its holster.

For propped up on a bunk beside the stove, one leg in rude splints, sat Pete Peralta. A hollow eyed, gaunt cheeked, unshaven Pete.

"Sam! Sam Graybull!" His voice was like the hoarse call of a crow. But there was a prayer in its welcome, as he voiced the name of the killer.

From the bedroom beyond came a broken, moaning sob. A woman's sob. A woman half delirious with pain.

"Horse fell and busted my leg . . . About a week ago . . . Rose took care of me until she had to quit . . . She's goin' to have a baby—and no doctor inside a hundred miles. I reckon she'll die."

It took Sam Graybull some seconds to comprehend fully. A pint or more of raw whisky on an empty stomach does not make for quiet thinking. The fact that he could retain even a semblance of his faculties proved the toughness of the killer.

"Doctor, eh?" Sam Graybull pushed back his muskrat cap and ran blunt fingers through his shock of coarse black hair. "Doctor? Yeah, you sure need one, don't you, Pete?"

"Not me, Sam. Her. She's out of her head, kinda."

"Dyin', Pete?"

"She will, I reckon. There has to be a doctor when a baby comes."

Sam Graybull passed his hand across his eyes. He knew nothing of childbirth. There had never been room in his killer's heart for sympathy for man or woman. Life and the losing of life meant but little to him. He nodded, black brows knit in a thoughtful scowl. Then he stepped outside and brought in the jug.

He poured three drinks into tin cups.

"Do us all good, Pete. Then we'll kinda figger this thing out." He took one of the cups and went into the next room.

"Howdy, Rose. Git outside o' this. Nothin' like it to kill pain."

Dimly, through eyes that were mere slits of red, he saw the white face of the girl. White as the pillow against the mass of black hair. He lifted her head and held the cup against the lips that seemed drained of blood.

"The pain--the pain. . ."

"Hell, ain't it? But that drink'll do you good."

He went back into the other room and handed Pete his cup.

"Here's luck, Pete. Down 'er. More where that come from."

Sam gulped down his drink without a grimace. His brain seemed to be clearing.

"Where do you keep your pencil and paper, Pete?"

"That shelf. God, Sam, if we could only do somethin' to help her."

"Keep your shirt on." Sam found the writing pad and pencil. He handed them to the crippled man.

"Write a note to the doctor, Pete. Tell it scary." Sam pulled on his cap again. "I'll be ready by the time you git it wrote."

"Where you goin', Sam?"

"Out to saddle up the best horse you got. I'm goin' fer the doctor. I'll stop by the nearest ranch and have 'em send over somebody to ride herd on you." The door banged shut behind him.

Sam caught Pete's best horse. When he had saddled the animal, he came back inside.

"Got that note finished?"

"Yes. But you can't make it into town, Sam."

"The hell I can't. The storm's quit. I know the road, and I ain't so drunk but what I kin ride. Lemme have that pencil."

He scrawled something at the foot of the note. Then he folded the paper and put it into his pocket.

"Hang and rattle, Pete, till the doc gits here." He poured some of the whisky into an empty vinegar bottle and put the corked bottle into his overcoat. Then he filled the two cups.

"Here's how, Pete. If the kid looks like you, I shore feel sorry fer the critter."

Sam tossed down his drink and before Pete Peralta could say a word, he was gone.

III

It was almighty hard luck, the way things had turned out for a man. When the only friend a man had was laid up with a busted laig and a sick wife. No "Red River Jig". No fire to set by. No Pete to talk to and tell how comical that bank dude looked when he dropped. No warm grub. Only that bottle. Better drop past the cabin and fill a jug. When a man ain't slept ner et he'd orter have a jug along to keep him alive.

He stopped at his cabin long enough to fill the jug. Then he pulled out. He rode into a Long X line camp. A slit eyed, frost blackened man who staggered a little when he walked. The two cowpunchers stared hard at him.

"Peter Peralta's in bad shape. Broke a laig. His missus is dyin'. I'm ridin' fer a doctor. One o' you boys git over there and look after things."

He wolfed some meat and beans and gave them a shot out of his jug. One of the cowpunchers was getting ready for the trip to Pete's. Sam Graybull climbed back into the saddle and rode on.

The storm had quit. The stars glittered like white sparks against the clear sky. The moon pushed up over the ragged ridges. Sam Graybull swayed a little as he rode, half asleep, half awake, back along the trail to town.

He took some tobacco and rubbed it into his eyes to sting them open. Now and then he took a drink from the jug. Not as big a drink as he wanted. Just enough to keep a man alive. That grub made a man sleepy. A paunch full of meat always made a man sleepy. Almighty hard luck that a man couldn't git off and lay down. For five minutes. Yeah. Five hours. Be froze stiff as a stick. Hadn't he froze his feet thataway? Wouldn't he a-died there only Pete come by? Hell, he was payin' Pete back right now. A man paid his debts thataway. Took guts, too. But when a man's got one friend on earth, he'd be a hell of a kind of man not to lend a hand. It took guts. Somethin' Pete didn't have. Pete was a chicken hearted cuss. With his wife and his fiddle. Never taken a chance. Never would get nowhere. Like a cow pasture. A muley cow. Well, no man had ever sawed Sam Graybull's horns. No fence made ever held him. No jail, neither. Never bin ketched. Them as tried it had some hard luck. Have a drink. Damn that cork. A man's hands stiff and numb. There she comes. Good whisky. Thawed a man's belly. Fightin' whisky.

Sam Graybull's laugh grated on the silence of the winter night. There'd be fightin' a-plenty if a man run into that fool posse. Sam took a beaded buckskin pouch and put into it the note to the doctor. Then he fastened the pouch around his neck outside his coat. He moved with a dogged, sluggish precision. Like a machine that needs oil. He lost one of his mittens. The right mitten. He put the other mitten on his right hand, leaving the left one bare. Sam Graybull's right hand was his gun hand.

Out of the hills and onto the main road to town. Daylight now. Sleepy. Dozing in the saddle. Ridin' that horse like he owned him. Payin' off the only debt he owed to his only friend.

Yonder was Beaver Crick. Old gray wolf a-comin' outa the bare willers. With a belly full of meat, headin' fer a safe place to sleep it off.

Sam never killed a wolf. Hell, he was a wolf, hisself. A he-wolf. A killer. No rabbit, like Pete Peralta. Pete, whinin' over a busted laig. What'd he do if he had a .30-.40 slug in him and had to gouge it out with a jacknife? Sam Graybull had done that.

What's a-comin' yonder? Horsebackers. A dozen er more. Posse men. Time fer a drink. A big'n this time. No nibble. Bin holdin' off. Waitin'.

"Here's lookin' at you boys!" Sam Graybull's hoarse voice carried a note of triumph. "Here's lookin' at you acrost gun sights!" And he left the fiery stuff gurgle down his throat.

A rifle bullet whined past Sam Graybull's head. He taunted the marksman with a yell of derision and, tossing aside the jug, jerked his carbine and rode at a run straight for the men.

A hail of bullets met his rush. Sam Graybull's horse somersaulted, shot between the eyes. Sam tried to kick his feet from the stirrups. Too late. Horse and man crashed together. A dull pain shot through the killer's leg. That leg was pinned under the dead weight of the horse. Bullets spatted and droned. Sam Graybull emptied his carbine. Two of the posse felt the searing sting of the outlaw's bullets. Sam pulled his six-gun—the .45 that had taken deadly toll of human life. His thumb fanned the hammer.

"Come an' git it! Come on, you red necks!"

Black lips bared from tobacco stained teeth. Slit eyes swollen almost shut. It took guts.

Something white hot stabbed Sam Graybull's chest. He hardly felt it. Above the flat spat of rifles in the dawn, sounded the mirthless laugh of Sam Graybull. A laugh that sounded like the death rattle. Tumbing the hammer of an empty gun. Then the weary head dropped back into the snow. Sam Graybull, killer, was dead.

The last of the whisky gurgled out of the uncorked jug into the trail.

"He must have got drunk, blind drunk, and lost his way."

"The sheriff pulled the dead outlaw clear of the horse. Grimly triumphant, the grizzled old officer examined the body of the killer. Then he opened the pouch and found the note.

As he read it, there in the sunrise of that winter morning, the warm glow of victory chilled. He turned to a man who carried a small black bag instead of a gun.

"This is fer you, Doc. You're wanted down on the river." He handed over the note. Then he turned to his men.

"Handle Sam easy, boys. He come back a-purpose, to do the only decent thing he ever done in his life. Pete Peralta's wife is about to have a baby. Sam Graybull come to fetch Doc. Handle 'im easy."

The sheriff and Doc Steele rode along the trail together. Doc read aloud the postscript to Pete Peralta's note.

"The bank money is in a sack under the hay at my cabin. What bounty there is on my hide goes to Pete Peralta. If the kid's a boy, name him Graybull. Use the bounty money to educate him. So long"

—SAM GRAYBULL.

And so it was that Doc Steele brought into the world a boy named Graybull Peralta. Some of the A.E.F. will remember him as Captain Graybull Peralta, the fighting chaplain of the —th Division, made up of men from the cow country. He was killed in action in the Argonne. In the pocket of his blouse was a bullet drilled, blood soaked Bible. In his hand was a bone handled six-gun with six notches filed on its age yellowed handle.

Major Steele, who found him, gently removed the empty gun from the dead captain's hand. He looked with memory misted eyes at the face of the fighting parson. The bared lips, the swollen, slitted eyes.

"Handle him gently, men," he told the stretcher bearers. "Gently, as we handled his father twenty years ago. May the son of Sam Graybull find fat meat in the Shadow Hills!"

And they were too busy, those stretcher bearers, to wonder at the queer words of the white haired surgeon.

The Loner

ROY NORTON

The times of John Barton are gone, although there still live in the Far West men with gray beards, halting steps and numbered days who can, from the somewhat dusty archives of memory, recall him. The type of men like John Barton seems also to have gone—unless, as ghosts, they haunt the trails that have grown dim or become obliterated through lack of use or utility. The very land that knew John Barton has changed from windswept valleys of grass, or deserts that needed but irrigation, to well-ordered farms tilled by a generation to whom a buffalo or a wild steer is as foreign as an animal in a menagerie. Of John Barton nothing but the legend remains. Not even those ancients with rheumy eyes from which the frontier keenness and alertness have long faded can tell whence he came, or what his antecedents; nor are these pertinent, for it is of what he did that they remember, and perhaps garrulously boast as if to prove to their grandchildren that their own brilliant days of lusty manhood were more virile, more stirring, more testing than these humdrum times of lethargic peace.

It was in those "days now dead beyond recall"—thank God!—that into the then straggling street of Big Cañon wandered John Barton, tall, bent, yet active despite gray hair and white beard. Hands and face were gnarled, but his eyes were keen, gray and of a disarming benevolence. He spoke but little, and always in a gentle voice, a voice that seemed to protest against anything harsh or sudden. He appeared content with the sole friendship of a dog. And the dog seemed equally content with the sole friendship of John Barton; for it was ever at his heels, or by his side when he sat down, and the gnarled hand invariably came to rest on the dog's head. Men observed the dog as much as its master; for it was a huge mongrel whose ancestry at some time had included a timber wolf. It resented its master's intercourse with other men, eying the entire world askance as if anticipating malevolence.

It had unquestionably been trained to guard John Barton's back; for whenever the man stopped in the street, the dog would instantly fall behind him, face the other way and keep vigilant watch. Once a man, imbued with friendliness, started to lay a hand on John Barton's shoulder—and there came through the air like a bolt of gray wrath, with huge fangs exposed and great head outthrust, that dog. Nothing save the quick thrust of Barton's arm saved the ripping of a man's throat, and provoked the only explanation he, John Barton, was ever known to give of his former life.

"Don't blame him, sir. —Down, Sioux! Get behind me! —He thought maybe you was goin' to go for me. You see, me and him's been in a country where we had to sort of look out for each other when the corners were tight, and—he meant nothin' by it—saved my life more'n once, and—"

His low, gentle voice died away into mumbled, inaudible, broken sentences, an habitual closure; but after that, the reputation of the dog called Sioux was established, and men moved with caution when in its vicinity. Yet dog and man had what was the extreme virtue of their days and environment, in that each strictly, unendingly, resolutely, "minded his own business."

The "business" of John Barton, it became known, was cattle. A cow-man might have denied this and called him, contemptuously, "a nester;" but he was the forerunner of those who knew how to farm as well as "run stock,' and most of all, knew how to depend upon themselves entirely and adequately. Big Cañon, being a divisional headquarters, caught the gossip of railway crews that the company had been induced to build a small cattle-pen and chute at Manipa; and men smiled and wondered, because Manipa, the first station west of Big Cañon, and eighty miles distant, had theretofore consisted of but three structures, a tiny red station, a huge, round water-tank, and a patchwork hovel for the section gang. Yet in due time three carloads of young stock consigned to John Barton were by him and Sioux driven away.

It was Tom Horn, the somewhat inquisitive storekeeper from whom John Barton bought his supplies, who first gleaned information of the latter's situation, hopes and emprise, with which he seemed content.

"It's like this," he explained in an unusual outburst of confidence. 'Most of my life I've been lookin' for a place that would just suit me so's I could settle down, quit driftin', an' call it home. Every man wants a home. Sometimes he finds it soon; sometimes he travels far, and if he's unlucky, sometimes never finds it at all—never! I've found mine. Long Valley, between rocks so high there's only two ways of gettin' in and out of it, and both so narrer they can be shut in with a fence; river through the middle; good grazin' for more cattle than I can ever own; some timber up in the hills; Manipa only twenty miles away; no bad Injuns and no bad neighbors..... Peace. Place where a man can sleep without hangin' onto his gun. What better could me and Sioux, after all we've been through—ummh—want than that? Huh? He likes it, and says he: 'Me and you are gettin' old, and damn' tired of shiftin', so let's stay here.' And I told him I would. So there him and me'll stick..... Home."

And Horn swore that the great dog that had arisen from between its master's feet, as if rendered apprehensive by such length of speech, suddenly smiled, licked the one hand it knew and loved in all the world, sighed deeply, and again rested content.

"But—wasn't there any place you could find nearer than that?" the storekeeper demanded, and then added, whimsically: "Seems to me you're a hell of a long way from anywhere."

"Me and Sioux are loners," John Barton mumbled thoughtfully, "and are used to bein' a hell of a long way from anywhere, so we don't like too damn' much company."

"Then I reckon that place ought to suit you," Horn agreed, with a grin, as he prepared to take Barton's orders. And from that day onward, with the aptitude for distinguishing appellations that characterized those times, old John Barton was known as "the Loner." Moreover for nearly two years he came, and went, sometimes accompanied by Sioux, more times alone, without men knowing more of him, his ways, or his accomplishments. Veritably a "loner." Save that it seemed his desire, pathetically alone.

Then in a single day, Barton came to local fame. Tempted by the sight of a prize rifle that he saw in Horn's window, which he fondled, mumbled over, and admired when told that it was as perfect a weapon as could be made, he succumbed to the storekeeper's facetious urging to "stay in town till the Fourth and win her." He borrowed Horn's rifle and spent a day in the hills "Gettin' the hang of her," and "to see if she's like my own at home." The jest spread broadcast, inasmuch as it was practically a border championship event, to be participated in by some then famous marksmen. On that eventful day his appearance was greeted with a roar of laughter, to which he was oblivious—more so indeed than the dog at his heels, which raised an angry ruff, then stared upward at the Loner as if expecting the latter speedily to punish that derision.

"Go it, Granddad!" was the way the umpire started the Loner off. The good-humored badinage from the crowd stopped after the fifth consecutive bull's-eye. It gave way to admiration at the seventh, provoked murmurs of applause at the ninth and burst into a wild cheer at the tenth. The Loner was too much engaged in pacifying Sioux to give heed. The distance-tests left him well in the lead, but the crowd was almost unanimous in its agreement that at rapid-fire, short-distances, a man of his age had small chance. The comments were audibly expressed. The umpire and both the famous experts protested, one of the latter whirling savagely round and shouting: "Men, you've seen this man Barton do some wonderful shooting. Give him a chance! It's not fair to talk when a man is on such a strain."

The Loner turned, and his clear eyes twinkled as he said: "Thank you, sir. But me and Sioux don't care. A lot of our shootin's been done where a feller couldn't afford to let noise make him miss—but—thanks just the same."

And then at the signal he threw the borrowed rifle up and with startling accuracy and rapidity made his score. The visiting experts were the first to congratulate him; for despite his years and an unfamiliar weapon, he was point to point with them in the final test, and the prize rifle was his. He had not known that a trophy cup, heavy and ornate, accompanied it, and seemed puzzled when the judges handed it to him. He took it in his big, rough hands, examined it, and slowly a look of profound disappointment settled on his face.

"It's purty," he said, "mighty purty; and thank you kindly, sir. But what do I have to do now to win that there rifle?"

"You've won it also. It was merely an additional prize. Here it is."

The Loner's face was gladdened swiftly as if by sunshine. He clutched the desired rifle to his breast while holding the borrowed firearm in the hollow of his arm. And then, with the silver cup, coveted by experts, dangling carelessly from a finger and bumping his leg, he said, "Come on, Sioux," and made his way out through the now adulatory crowd. He went to Horn's store and patiently awaited the storekeeper's return while the bewildered clerks whispered their astonishment.

"Mr. Horn," the Loner said when the storekeeper, imbued with a new respect, returned, "you was right kind to me. That's a good gun of yours. I reckon you'd not lend her to anybody but a friend. This cup thing—can't drink out of it—no use—aint touched a drop in more'n twenty year, and—" He scratched his chin in perplexity and then brightened as he asked: "You got a woman? Yes? Well, give it to her. Women seem most always to like things that are purty, but no use."

***

When Horn attempted to make him appreciate the value of the trophy, he appeared unimpressed and in a burst of magnanimity said: "It was right selfish of me! I ought to have let you take your choice. Would you rather have the rifle?"

"Of course not. I'd rather have the cup!"

"Then there it is on the counter—no, on the floor. Forgot just where I put it, but— I wouldn't have said nothin', but I'd sure have been disappointed if you'd picked the gun. Always did want to have the finest rifle in the world—never expected—seems like— Git down, Sioux!...."

His words died away as they frequently did, in the folds of his white beard, as if smothered by long repression, loneliness, ineptitude, until utterance seemed waste.

When he went out of the store, one of the clerks laughed, and to his astonishment Horn turned and snapped: "Shut up! There's goin' to be no more jokes about that old man. He put his hand in mine when he told me we were friends. I took it. From now on, anybody who makes fun of him answers to me. I was a damn' fool myself; for, I tell you, even if he don't look up to much, the Loner's a great old man. I saw it in his eyes. He's got something inside of him that counts."

The evidence of trust imposed in Horn by the Loner was not long in forthcoming. It took form in a check which Barton had received for his first shipment of cattle, and was inclosed with a letter:

I don't like banks. One busted once and busted me. So I wish you'd get the money for this here piece of paper and keep it in your safe till I want it.

John Barton.

P. S. You can use it if you want to till I want to use it, which'll most likely not be before next spring.

Spring came, indeed, before the Loner called on Horn.

"Goin' to buy some young stuff to run and fatten," he explained.

"John, you can have your money any time you want it," said Horn, "but have you heard about this bunch of rustlers called the Birch Gang? Well, they're a bad lot. It's pretty generally known that they're running whole herds of stock off the range, but so far, no one has been able to prove it on them—that is, if anyone has, he's turned his toes up before he got a chance. Nobody knows that they committed murder, but there's a dozen men been found dead that can't be accounted for. A United States deputy marshal told me confidentially, only last week, that they've been working in Wyoming until it got too hot for them, and that they're thought to have come this way. If I were you, I'd go slow on cattle until this gang is wiped out, or we can be sure they're not out near your range."

The Loner was influenced, and depressed.

"Seems tough luck on me," he remarked. "I done so well out of that last lot, and—why, I was just sayin' to Sioux the other night that maybe we'd have to hire a feller to help us, and buy some farm horses and a plow. We thought of a few pigs and chickens, too, and—I don't know— Rustlers! Bumped into some of 'em—Canadian border—thought we'd got to—everything so peaceful-like and—"

The storekeeper did not catch the final words, but feeling a great sympathy for this lonely and trustful old man, gave more advice:

"I'd put that money out at interest, and be contented with that for a while. The law will get the Birch Gang sooner or later, and—"

"But I'm only' runnin' a bunch of about a hundred now, and—interest? I don't know nothin' about such things. I never had to borrow money, and until now it seems like I never had none to lend."

"Well, all I can say is that even a hundred head of stock is enough to make the Birch Gang move your way if it comes handy. I'd sell them too, if I were you, and wait until things blew over. You're not too young, and you're a long way from anywhere. The nearest neighbor you've got is twenty miles away, and after that not a one nearer than here. I'm not too much of a coward, but—if I was as far from neighbors as you are, I'm not certain but that I'd move out for a while."

Horn went on to tell other gruesome stories of the Birch Gang, of the fact that even sheriffs were not too keen to hunt them, and of the terror which their murderous lawlessness had spread over the range. The Loner sat on a cracker box for more than an hour, his shoulders drooped a little more than usual, his head bent forward, his big hands listless, his whole attitude one of disappointment and depression. He finally agreed, after much more persuasion, to consider the matter for a few weeks longer, but could not be induced to seek a safer situation.

"No, Horn," he said, finally, "I don't allow to be scared out of the country. And maybe they're not in my neck of the woods at all. Maybe they'll not come. I'm sort of out of the way—"

"Out of the way—nothing! You're in exactly the line they'd take if they undertook to run bunches of rustled stock toward the southern border. The Maldai Pass is in a line due south of you, and the open range north! You've got a closed valley where they could lay low and round up rustled steers. You've got the only water and grass in a hundred-mile circle."

"Just the same, I'm goin' back there to stay. Me and Sioux likes it there. It's the first real home me and him's had for years, and—maybe it's all talk and—couldn't find us most likely—no regular trails—hard goin'—ought to have some luck after—"

His voice died away as usual into murmurs; but awhile later he gave his usual order for supplies and promised to return within six weeks.

Dejected, he sat alone in the westbound train that night, seeming to find no interest in the half-dozen other occupants of the coach, and but little in the conversation of the brakeman, who recognized him, and dropped into the seat by his side for a chat.

"Aint you afraid the rustlers will give you a visit, Uncle John?" the young man asked. "We heard on the up-trip that some of the runs a little west of you are missing a lot of steers."

"Nope," the Loner insisted, stubbornly, "they aint likely to come my way."

The brakeman shook his head at such optimism, and, suddenly remembering that Manipa station was near, got up and hurried through the train bawling the name as if expecting that other passengers than the Loner might wish to get off at such an isolated, out-of-the-world stop. None did. The Loner got off alone, went to the rear of the section house where it was his custom to leave his pack-burro and saddle-pony, collected his meager supplies that had been dumped off the train, made his pack, and rode away over the waste of sand and sagebrush into the late afternoon glow.

Off on the horizon the bleak hills began to appear clear-cut as iron teeth against the skyline, and his patient eyes were fixed on them with the yearning of the wanderer, homeward bound. Great, friendly shapes they were to him, for there, in their heart, lay his valley of dreams and attainment. He talked to his burro now and then, and the long gray ears would stop their listless waving as if to listen and understand,

"Cain't you walk a little faster, Pete? Roney, here, under me aint satisfied with you goin' so slow. We got to get home sometime, you know."

And Pete seemed to quicken his steps, and the saddle-pony to move less impatiently. The desert gave way to sand dunes, to patches of barren, protruding rocks, and finally to stony foothills through which the little cavalcade wound its way with the certainty of familiarity. The hoofs lost their shuffle, and struck sparks from stones. A tiny forest of scrub pines that for decades had fought to subsist was passed; the hot air no longer rippled upward, weaving fantastic gyrating figures in a blur, and the moist smell of water came to the red and dilated nostrils. They came out on a cliff at a spot from which with caution they could descend, and there, nestled below them in the purple haze, rested the cabin and the clumsy outbuildings surrounded by the sea of grass, green with the tender color of spring, but now, in the dusk, a carpet of pale emerald.

The Loner always stopped there and whistled, waiting to hear the distant deep-throated welcome of that loyal watchman left on guard. Always his face took on an expectant and mild glow of enjoyment in anticipation of that sound. It was so on this night of his return. But it proved unlike other nights, for there was no immediate response. Nothing at first but a silence, filled only with the croon of the evening breeze through the pines.

"That's strange—mighty strange," he muttered, and whistled again, listening attentively for a reply. It came at last, in a plaintive, weak yelp, as if Sioux had been compelled to exhaust his powers in a single sound which, faithful to the last, he must utter though it be beyond his strength.

Alarmed, John Barton urged his pony recklessly down the trail that wound back and forth the face of the cliff. And then he saw, crawling toward him with dragging hind legs, and uttering plaintive whines, that strange partner of his, the great mongrel dog. The Loner flung himself from his saddle crying, "Sioux! Sioux! What is it?" He dropped to his knees and caught the dog in his arms. The dog rested there, licking the gnarled hands with hot tongue, whimpering a tale of distress and defeat—endeavoring to explain his first great failure, and his fierce but hopeless fight.

"Shot by God! He's been shot three times!" The Loner's voice arose in an excited and angry exclamation. He gathered the dog farther into his arms, and strode toward the cabin muttering words of sympathy, of anger, and of endearment, all in broken phrases, detached, confused, and burdened with his great distress. The pony trudged sympathetically at his heels, unheeded. Behind came the burro, as if intent on sharing this tragic episode.

Barton carried the dog in and laid it on his own bed, before thinking it strange that the door of the cabin should be standing wide. He lit the lamp and looked around. The place was in disorder. A meal had been cooked, and the table was littered with the unwashed enameled plates and broken food. And in the middle of its wreckage, like an upright survivor of debauch, stood an empty whisky-bottle in which was stuck a fork holding a sheet of paper torn from the front of old John Barton's Bible. He held it beneath the lamp and read:

Your little bunch of stock is gone because we can use them. Your dog is dead because he was a fool and didn't know when to quit fighting. So take warning. Clear out of this, and clear for good. If we catch you here again when we come through this way, you'll get the same the dog got, which was plenty. And if you are wise, you wont make too much talk about why you left either, because you'll be got if you do.

The Gang.

For a minute Barton stood, bewildered by this enormity, this unmerited enmity, this tragic downfall of his house of peace. His tired old eyes swept the walls of his abode reproachfully, as if they had deserted him and no longer afforded security. The familiar objects had been knocked about by ruthless, wanton hands, curious perhaps, or even malevolent. The sturdy old clock that he had prized had been used as a target, and its brass bowels protruded in melancholy ruin. His mind wandered in aimless, stricken circles, beginning nowhere, ending nowhere, and then slowly steadied. He observed that there had been seven plates used from that proud store of his purchased in distant Big Cañon at an auction sale.

As he gazed, the dog moaned and twisted on the bed. Instantly all else was forgotten. He trudged hastily across the room.

"Sioux!" he said. "Poor old boy! Seven of 'em you fought! Fought 'em all until they thought they'd got you! My God! How I wish I'd been here with you!"

He heard a noise at the open door, and saw that both Roney and Pete were standing with their heads inside, wondering at his forgetfulness and lack of care, their eyes wide with reproach and bewilderment. Apologizing in a steady flow of words, he went to them, took off pack and saddle, and told them to go and help themselves to a drink and food. He tried clumsily to dress the dog's wounds, bathing them with warm water, examining them, and shaking his head and muttering doubtfully; but Sioux, as if soothed by his presence, merely lay more quietly with dumb, agonized eyes following his movements.

Barton cleaned away the table, prepared himself some food, and ate it like an automaton, for his mind was bewildered with shock. In the midst of his meal he remembered that fabulous rifle of his, that most cherished of possessions, and crawled under his rough bunk with outstretched hands, feeling for it in the place where he always kept it, not for concealment alone, but for dryness and care. He brought it out, swathed in woolen rags and cotton, and patted it with his hands and spoke to it, congratulating it upon its escape. Once more he attended that stricken companion of his, and stood above the bunk scratching his chin through his white beard as if to stimulate resource for such a terrible emergency.

Then suddenly he bent forward and said: "Sioux, it's goin' to be a hard trip, but I reckon we'll have to have a doctor. You see, I aint much good at this sort of thing, so you'll have to put up with it till we can get you somewhere. You really ought to be put in one of them hospertals. I'll go out and git Roney now."

At one o'clock in the morning the lone agent at Manipa was aroused from sleep by the Loner, who carried in his cramped arms, as if it were an injured child, a half-conscious dog, while slung over his shoulder was a burnished rifle.

"Wh—wh—what the hell's this?" the sleepy agent demanded, opening his eyes and staring at the white-bearded old man who peered at him appealingly.

"It's me—John Barton. Sioux's been hurt bad. Shot! You can stop trains, cain't you? They'll stop if you ask 'em with that red light of your'n, wont they?"

The agent protested, disdainfully, volubly, with that official impatience which reaches its worst in only such a station as his. The appeal died from the visitor's eyes and gave way to something hard and stern.

"You say you cain't stop a train without orders. Well, I order you to stop the next one that comes through and—you'll do it, too. If you don't—"

His disengaged hand swept upward and patted the barrel of the rifle.

"I mean it!" he declared grimly. "I take Sioux on the next train."

He did. It was a fast freight with trundling refrigerator-cars hurrying fruits from distant Western shores to Eastern markets, and the conductor swore turbidly and threatened to report until he too was overawed by the grim old man with rifle and with dog. Yet that report was never made; because on that long, tedious journey which John Barton was making for the second and unexpected time, the conductor heard the story, sympathized, and cursed still more volubly with oaths directed at the perpetrators of such an outrage. He proffered advice:

"There's only one veterinarian in Big Cañon, Doc' Mathews," he said. "And I'm not sure that he knows much about dogs; but he's there when it comes to horses and other livestock. A regular human doctor don't know anything about dogs, I reckon. Go to Mathews."

And at five o'clock that morning Mathews was visited by the man with the dog, gun and rifle. While the veterinary examined his patient, Sioux, with mysterious animal intuition, evidently sensed that he was in the hands of a friend, for he submitted to probings and dressings without baring a fang.

"If you ask me," the veterinarian said to the silent old man, "that dog is pretty badly shot to pieces. It would be a mercy to put him out of his misery, because if you don't, he'll most likely be a cripple for life, partially paralyzed."

"Good Gawd!" said the Loner indignantly, and with wide eyes. "Is that any reason to kill a friend? Why, that's the time to stick to him through thick and thin. You don't reckon Sioux would help kill me if I were paralyzed, do you? Nosir-ee! He aint that kind of a feller, and I aint either. If you pull him through, the price don't matter. I aint rich, but I'll give all I got." And then, as his losses dawned on him, he qualified it with: "All I got left."

"Well, leave the dog here, and be sure I'll do all I can for him," Mathews said, and deftly inserted a hypodermic injection of morphia to ease the animal's pain, then showed its owner to the door.

When the sheriff came to open his office in the county courthouse, he discovered a tired old man sitting on the courthouse steps, asleep. The sheriff stared curiously, and then said: "Blessed if it isn't old John Barton—the Loner."

The exclamation awoke the sleeper, who got to his feet and said: "Been waitin' for you, Sheriff."

And as they passed inside, he told of his disaster. The sheriff scowled and clenched his fists when the story was finished, then glared at the written notice issued by the rustlers.

"John," he said kindly, "I wish I could go after them. The Lord knows I do! It's undoubtedly the Birch Gang, and from now on there'll be trouble around here; but don't you understand that I'm hog-tied like a thrown steer? This is Colorado. You belong in another State, and another county, and I'm not allowed to cross over into Utah to run down cattle-thieves. You should have gone to the sheriff of your county."

"But—but my county's several hundred miles square, and the sheriff is almost a day's journey by train!"

Again the sheriff sadly shook his head and said: "I know it is. And I know that to bring a posse so far takes time and money, and that before it could be done, those steers of yours would probably have been shipped and the thieves starting out to rustle a fresh batch. That's what makes it possible for that Birch Gang to get away with all they do. They're not much afraid of the law in a country like this. All they're afraid of are the cattle-men themselves. It's almost impossible under the law to get them! It's an outrage, but it can't be helped. I don't honestly know what you can do about it. If you had neighbors that could band together to help one another, you might make it too hot for them. That's what they did up on the Wyoming ranges, and that's why the gang's come down into this country. But one thing I'll tell you: if I were you, I'd take that warning mighty seriously, and not go back until, somehow or another, that gang of rustlers is wiped out. It's as much as your life is worth, I tell you, to try to stick there. What does the murder of one lonely man, away off by himself, amount to to them? Nothing! Not as much as that!" And he snapped his fingers.

The Loner sat for a long time brooding helplessly before he said: "Then it seems there aint anything at all that I can do. The law can't help me so—my stock is gone and—they'll take my ranch to use for a roundup of stolen stock."

"That's about it," the sheriff admitted. "But of course, if I were you, I'd get on the train and go out to your own county seat and lay the case before the sheriff. I've met him several times. He's a good man and will do the best he can. But I don't hold out any hope, and he wont, of doing much. I'll give you a letter to him, so he'll know that when you tell him a thing he can be sure it's gospel truth, and—that a lot of us over here like to call you a friend."

But Barton did not travel westward. Disconsolate, harassed, hurt and helpless, he explained the situation to Horn:

"First, it seems it wouldn't get me nowhere, and second, I couldn't leave nohow on account of Sioux. I'm mighty anxious about Sioux. If he don't get well, I don't know what on earth I'll do. I don't see how I could ever get along without him, now. And he cain't get well without me. And besides, if he don't, I wouldn't have him cash in his chips thinkin' I'd deserted him. That'd be the worst of all. Friendship is friendship, and never yet have I thrown down a friend."

And so for eight anxious days Barton wandered like a lost ghost here and there, sometimes far out into the mountains, sometimes through the streets, always unseeing, as if his troubled old eyes were looking into a perplexed and unpromising future; and for hours each day he sat in the sunshine outside the veterinarian's stables with one hand resting on the back of a dying dog. When the end came, he picked the big body up gently, as if still hoping for a responsive recognition from something that in all its faithful life had never failed, carried it out into the hills and, muttering his grief, buried it and made a cairn of rocks to mark the grave.

Tired from his labors, he sat down beside the rough monument, took off his hat, wiped the sweat from his forehead, and stared off at the tops of the distant snow-bound peaks as if communing with them. At last the old lips beneath the white beard tightened and he stood up. "Good-by, Sioux!" he said. "Where you are now you're all right. Don't worry none about me. I'll just have to get along without you, somehow. Good-by!"

He spoke with the solemnity of conviction—his conviction that God in heaven couldn't be so unkind as to leave dogs like Sioux unsouled and with all their life's fidelity unrewarded after death. The thought comforted him as with firm steps he walked to the town on the plateau below. Just as Horn was closing his store that night, Barton entered.

"John," he said, "I came to buy a lot of cartridges and to say good-by. I'm goin' home on the train that goes through here at three o'clock in the mornin'."

Horn, aghast at such folly, sat down and tried to dissuade him; but his words beat as uselessly as a wind against a peak.

"I know—just as you say—that the law cain't help me," said the Loner, "so from now on I'll help myself. It's all the home I got, and I'm goin' to stay there, dead or alive."

"Then you'll probably stay there dead!" Horn exclaimed, exasperated by such unreasoning stubbornness, and bade him not "Good-by," but "Farewell."

When he took his seat in the train, the Loner attracted no attention; for at that hour travelers slept, sprawling in their seats beneath the half-dimmed lights in an atmosphere that was stale with many odors. And as if relaxed after a long vigil, the Loner slept too, until aroused by the brakeman who shook him to wakefulness. Hugging his rifle and a small bundle of supplies, he stepped off into the sand, blinking as if dazed, and then recovering wits and purposefulness, he went to the shed where his saddle-pony, wearied with long inactivity, whinnied a greeting. For the first time in days the old man smiled.

"That was good of you, Roney," he said, caressing the soft outthrust muzzle. "You and Pete's all I got left now. Sioux aint goin' to be with us no more."

He scanned the manger and the feed-box to make certain that the section men had not neglected the horse during his absence, and satisfied of this, saddled and led it to the foot of the great red tank, where he gave it water. He rode away as the east reddened and lent strange tints and beauties to the sands, the sage and the clean morning skies. But he rode without that wonderful sense of homecoming with which heretofore he had always taken the trail. In place of this kindly, warm emotion, his thoughts were grim, determined, troubled.

The sun was up when, with Roney breathing deeply and sweating from the upward climb, he came slowly out through the edge of the scrub pines to the first view of his cabin. And then he suddenly pulled his mount to a halt, and frowning, glared downward. A column of gray smoke was plumed upward in the still air like a pillar of pale light, and the cabin door was open, as were the shutters over the solitary window at the end. Two men with hats on the backs of their heads sat straddlewise on the homely bench whereon for so long he and Sioux had been accustomed to rest. They played cards as if wholly absorbed in pursuit of gain. Barton's eyes, stern and alert, shifted and swept over the visible portion of his valley. Strange cattle were there, resting as if they had been cruelly driven in the night or preceding day. Strange horses were there, and he counted them—seven. That telltale number! Seven, just as there had been seven of his plates used before his own herd had been driven away, and—the thought brought flame again to his eyes—when Sioux, faithful old Sioux, had fought to the death,

John Barton dismounted and carefully led Roney well back into the forest screen. He took the marvelous rifle into his hands with a new clutch, made certain that it was fully loaded, then undid his bundle, took from it a box of cartridges and emptied them into his coat pocket. He trudged unfalteringly back, then by a zigzag route and keeping behind cover—now a rock, now a clump of brush clinging precariously to the shelves of the cliff—gained a lower and closer altitude that commanded both door and window. He carefully selected a boulder over the tops of which grew in profusion a screen of brush He took off his coat as if going to manual labor, spread his cartridges within reach and then, resting on his knees behind the boulder, thrust his rifle through the screen, brushed his eyes as if to make certain of their clarity, took careful aim and fired. Nor had the echoes of the snapping report come back from across the valley before he fired again. Without a sound the two men who had been playing cards collapsed, as if actuated by common and timed impulse, fell sidewise, and lay twitching upon the beaten earth.

From the cabin door two men rushed into view, looking wildly around. And this time the two rifle reports were so close together that their echoes returned as one, and now there were four men making the last, convulsive, involuntary movements of abruptly extinguished life. Door and window of the cabin closed swiftly as if to shut out the sight; the grazing ponies lifted their heads and stared excitedly as if such sounds were familiar precedents for quirt-tormented speed, agonizing distances, and merciless rowels when they stumbled from exhaustion. The ensuing silence, augmented by contrast, protracted, reassured them, and they returned to their grazing.

Up behind the screen of boulder and brush John Barton rested patiently, calm, unmoved, unpitying, with the sights of the rifle trained upon the window.

"You showed no mercy to Sioux," he said as if his low-pitched soliloquy could reach listening ears, "and so I show none to you.'

He watched the window unblinkingly, persistently, expectantly.

"First of all," he reflected, "they'll wonder if they're surrounded. That's what they'll be afraid of. Afraid a posse's caught up with them at last. Then bimeby they'll take a chance on lookin' out to see, and they'll just naturally try the window first. There's three of 'em in there, sure! Most likely they was still in their blankets when I opened up. Maybe been ridin' hard last night. And then—"

He did not finish the sentence, but fired; and a spot of white that had cautiously appeared at the window was there no longer. Also the glass came rattling brokenly outward and fell tinkling on the bench below.

"I reckon I got that feller—and that as he went down, he flung his hands out and that's what smashed my window," the Loner reasoned. "It cost me a heap of trouble to get it out here and keep it unbusted, but that's just one thing more to charge up ag'in' this gang." He patted his rifle and murmured: "They said you was the best gun in the world, and I'm tellin' you now that they didn't lie none about you." He stroked its blue barrel affectionately, and resumed his meditation with: "Now, the other two that's left'll be too scared to move for a long time, and when they do, maybe they'll come through the door on the run."

For more than an hour the same silence, usually so filled with an assurance of peace, but now rendered ominous by the proofs of death stretched motionless outside the cabin, continued. Only the birds in the little forest at the top of the cliffs took heart and resumed the songs of mating spring. The Loner was annoyed by the delay.

"Aint you ever comin' out?" he growled. "I don't want to camp here forever. I want to get it over with so's I can go down and get my cabin cleaned up and see how much damage you've done this time."

If his mind could have commanded his enemies, they would have immediately responded by opening the door. But it did not. And so, after a time, he fell to a ruse that he had used in situations far more dangerous to himself than this—got a branch of brush, put his hat on it, got one arm behind him, cuddled his rifle aimed at the cabin with the other, and thrust the hat upward.

A streak of fire came from between the logs of the cabin where the chinking had been dug away to make a loophole. The Loner grinned and fired five shots as rapidly as he could pull the trigger, two at the loophole, two at the window, and one at the center of his door.

"Never thought of that before," he commented. "That door's one of them factory made things that a bullet from a first-class rifle like this here will shoot through like it was paper. I hate to spile that nice door, but—"

He poured a fusillade alternately through the door and the window, splintering the thin panels of the former, smashing the last cherished pane from the latter.

"If that'll only make them believe there's nobody here but me," he thought, "they'll probably take chances on a rush pretty soon." But in this he was disappointed. Furthermore, at the end of an hour he was puzzled by something unusual and not understandable. The smoke from the chimney, that had for a long time been but a slender spiral of heated blue, suddenly gave forth a cloud of steam. For a moment it puffed upward, dissipated, and thereafter there was neither steam nor smoke.

"Throwed water on the fire!" the Loner exclaimed at last as if triumphantly solving a deep problem. "Wonder what for they did that? It'll crack my nice iron stove! Seems like they just do all they can to be mean."

Faint but sharp metallic sounds came to his hearing after another wait, but for these he could find no explanation. The sun gained the meridian, poured showers of heat into the valley and over the face of the cliff, and yet from the cabin came no further sounds. Barton, reasoning slowly, decided that the men within might wait for darkness to escape. The thought for a moment angered him, and he cogitated the advisability of leaving his post, regaining the top of the cliff, traversing it for a mile, finding a way of descent, and then closing in to within shouting distance. He turned his head and looked back for a route of covered retreat. When he looked at the cabin again, he understood the reason for the strange actions and sounds that had baffled him. Where the window had been was something of lighter color than the solid black of a darkened interior.

"Damn 'em!" he growled. "They've done took my stove to pieces and fastened the top of it ag'in' my winder. They've plumb ruined it."

He took a shot at the steel barricade, and saw a splinter ripped loose from a log at the side, proving that the bullet had ricocheted, and that the shield was effective. It was that which decided him. With the caution and skill of a veteran Indian fighter and frontiersman, he retreated from cover to cover back up the hillside and to the top. Loath to lose time, lest his victims escape in the interval, he ran through the chaparral heedless of thorns, tearing the fabric of what he termed his "store clothes," gained a familiar place for the descent, and rapidly made his way downward. Once a treacherous rock betrayed him, and he fell eight or ten feet, heavily jarring a body no longer resilient with youth, and driving the breath from his lungs. For twenty minutes he rested there on his back, half-dazed, before he could recover—then the iron of his determination drove him on.

Keeping the outbuildings between him and the cabin, he lunged heavily up the valley until he gained his stable, where he paused to recover breath and rest his aches. He considered the advisability of demanding a surrender, and then remembered that from his vantage point he could cover neither door nor window. His problem was imperative by now, for already the sun was on the quick western lap, and soon the night would fall. And then he fell to cursing his own stupidity.

"Why did I ever come down here, anyhow?" he thought. "There's a full moon and she's as clear as day. They can't try the window to get out, because they've had to fasten that stove-top too solid to get it down without raising a row, so they'd have had to get out through the door. I'd have done better to have stayed up there in front of 'em."

He decided now that if his enemies chose to wait for night, he could do the same, but retreated until he gained the shelter of a little log storehouse from the corner of which he could keep watch upon the door. The time passed slowly, as if it too were bound in a spell—as if the sun were loath to continue its round until witnessing the finale of this lonely tragedy in such a lonely place. The birds sang their vesper songs and drowsily twittered in concluding gossip. Far up in the valley Pete brayed, the sound coming to his owner fraught with anxiety, or loneliness.

"Poor little cuss! He wonders what's become of me, and Roney, and Sioux," Barton thought as he lay there inflexibly, unremittingly intent on guarding the closed and splintered door. The sun, finally concluding its observation, resumed its perpetual duty and sank from sight. The night seemed filled with a silence that sighed with anxiety. The stars and great round moon, wan in the early dusk, became brilliant lights as the hours advanced, and the Loner thought of his cherished clock, wantonly ruined, and of how proud he had been of its chime beaten out with a brass hammer on a great spring wire.

"She was so loud and fine that if she was still runnin' I could hear her strike clean out here," he thought, almost boastfully, quite like one recounting the value of lost treasure. He remembered with a pang that Sioux had howled and barked, much to his master's amusement, for the first few times when the clock struck after it had been brought "home."

"And now he'll never bark again. Not even when I come back from a trip."

His lips quivered a little beneath his beard and then hardened savagely, remorselessly, when he considered that brutal injustice. There was no pity within him as he stolidly waited for the end.

It came unexpectedly, and from an unexpected quarter. From the opposite side, where the cabin cast a shadow like a sheet of black velvet on the grass, there came a noise so slight that to ears less acute than those of the pioneer it would have been inaudible. A low, softly scraping sound, stealthy, unavoidable.

"My Lord! It's the winder, after all!" the listening man muttered. He tensed himself for action, then heard a thud as of feet dropped upon the bench outside the cabin window. He waited no longer, but leaped to his feet and ran round the back of the cabin toward the corner, rifle in ready hands.

Two figures in swift motion emerged from the shadow, undoubtedly believing that the blind wall of the cabin was unguarded, and rushed upon him. The Loner fired from his hip, and one man shouted, threw his hands up and toppled backward, and a revolver hurled into the air caught blue glints from the moon. The second running figure fired, and the Loner stumbled to his knees. "Hit!" he muttered, but instantly fired again. He failed to bring down the man who had shot him. The fugitive whirled and fired again, and the kneeling man's hat flew outward like a black vulture of the night taking a short flight in expectancy of prey. Its loss disturbed the Loner's aim, and before he could shoot, his assailant was in flight again, and running toward the shelter of the shed. The Loner, still on his knees took what was for him a long and careful aim, and shot but once; for the runner suddenly bounded into the air, dipped his head forward, took a few more steps through convulsive impetus, and then came to the ground in a heavy somersault and lay there doubled grotesquely, like a gnome resting still in devout adoration of the moon. The Loner calmly got to his feet, paused to consider, fancied he saw movement in that huddled shape, and deliberately fired into it again. A noise behind him attracted his attention, and swiftly he turned, raising his rifle, as he did so.

"Don't shoot again! For God's sake, don't!" an anguished voice implored, and just in time the ready gnarled finger on the rifle trigger restrained itself.

The man first shot had gained a sitting posture and was doubled forward holding his arms tightly clenched across his abdomen.

"Throw your gun!" commanded the Loner.

"I haven't got it!"

"Then up with your hands. Quick!" There was neither compassion nor hesitancy in the harsh old voice. Nothing but the chill and willing readiness to inflict death. The man's hands went feebly aloft, and the Loner strode across to him, assured himself that no arms were at hand and then demanded: "Are there any more of you?"

"No. You've got us all! And none of us even got a chance at you but Tim Birch, him that lies out there by the shed."

"So that was Birch, eh? I'm glad now that I shot him twice. I wish to God he could have lived until I could have filled him full of lead—like he did to my dog. That's mainly why I came back the way I did. I hated to shoot them two outside because they wasn't armed, and then I remembered that Sioux wasn't armed, either."

"My God! You don't mean that you came back on account of a dog, and shot us down one after the other?"

"Just that! I could have got more steers. I could even have got another ranch; but I couldn't get another friend like Sioux!"

He spoke earnestly, as if justifying his remorselessness, his methods, his mental trepidations.

"I've killed plenty of men in my time," he added. "I never have liked to, but they was always trying to kill me, and it was always face to face; but—you fellers weren't worth a fair fight. You were a lot of damned cowards. Not worth my dog that you shot. And so—I shot you like coyotes!"

He paused, interrupted in his anathema by the groans and contortions of the man at his feet.

"After all," he said, softly, "I'm sorry I had to do it—now that it's done. I'm hit myself, through the leg, but you're bad hurt. I couldn't leave any wounded thing to suffer. Wait here, and I'll get into my cabin and light the lamp, then bring you in and see what I can do for you."

He went into the cabin, found the lamp and stared at the havoc about him. He held the lamp above a dead man on the floor beneath the window, and confirmed the accuracy of that shot fired—was it that morning, or many, many mornings since? Time had run laggardly throughout that direful day of battle. He saw the ruin of his stove and recovered the iron kettle from the floor and carried it outside with the intention of lighting a fire to heat water therein. He advanced to the wounded man, who was now stretched out and moaning like a hurt animal. It flashed through his mind that this sound was similar to that made by Sioux when the latter came to meet him with dragging hips and feet. The man muttered something about having sold his cattle with others "across the line;" and then, even as the Loner, relenting, strove to pick him up in his arms, gasped and lay inert.

The Loner, limping with his burden, carried it into the cabin and laid it on the bed; but his effort had been wasted, for the last of the Birch Gang was dead. In the light of the lamp Barton bound his own wound, which experience convinced him was painful but not dangerous, and then stood for a moment staring at the lamp.

"I got to get to Roney," he muttered. "He's been up there all day, but—" And then he blew out the lamp, closed the door softly as if fearing to disturb the dead, and with seeming absurdity painfully carried a pail of water in his hand when he limped away to the steeply climbing trail. He gave the horse the water, apologizing meantime in muttered sentences for his neglect; then, with difficulty getting into the saddle, he turned and rode away.

Once more the railway agent was aroused from midnight sleep by a battered summons, harsh, imperative, on his door. Once more he came out, complaining, and was silenced by the cold glare in the eyes that pinned his attention.

"I want to send a message and—"

"Can't you wait till morning?"

"I'm sending it now!" the Loner said, thrusting his face forward. "And you'll send it, young feller. Do I have to—"

The agent shrank back from that cold wrath and apologetically acquiesced. He lighted the lamp in front of his counter, afraid to protest, and stood while the Loner with much effort, and care, and many starts, stoppings and alterations, addressed a dispatch to his friend Horn. And the agent gasped when he read in that cramped hand:

Send by first train seven plain pine wood coffins. I've killed the Birch Gang, but as the law didn't help me do it, I aint goin' to bother no coroner. Also send one good iron cookstove and a winder sash reg'lar size, because I got to fix up my home.

The End

About the Authors

Harvey Stanbrough is a retired Marine and a prolific professional writer in Southeast Arizona. He adheres to Heinlein's Rules and writes into the dark. For a time, he wrote under a few personas and several pseudonyms, but he takes a pill for that now and writes only under his own name. In just over 8 years, Harvey has written over 95 novels, 9 novellas, and around 250 short stories across several genres. None of that is a typo. To see Harvey's fiction and nonfiction, please visit his discount store at https://payhip.com/StoneThreadPublishing. You might especially enjoy his Writing Better Fiction.

Blake Bobechko is the author of the traditionally-told and fully-illustrated animal fiction, Frog of Arcadia. He lives in Orangeville, Ontario with his wife and three children. From there, he is actively involved in children's ministry, building up young disciples for Christ. Blake loves fishing and camping, and always takes great joy in hearing from people who have enjoyed his writing. He can be reached through his website frogofarcadia.com or through his X account @Blake-Bobechko

Frank Kidd is an author and screenwriter living in Missouri. He writes across genres, but specializes in westerns and historical adventure. He is also a veteran, an outdoorsman, and an amateur historian. Some of his favorite authors include Louis L'Amour, Jack London, Richard Matheson, and Robert E. Howard. You can follow his work via his online publication, Pulp West.

Brady Putzke is a professional musician who has always had a deep love of the written word. Coupled with a passion for storytelling and an obsession with mastering the craft of fiction, he took to writing novels. Dream House is his debut. When he is not reading or writing for hours on end, you can usually find him listening to baroque music or some obscure death metal band. Brady lives in Arizona with his wife and daughter.

Gaius Warner is an author of (mostly!) speculative fiction from Birmingham, Alabama. He regularly publishes long and short projects on his Substack and YouTube channel entitled, "The Graveyard Orbit." His newest novella, Crawlspace, was released in 2024.

When not scribbling away at his next yarn, **London Baker** can be found wandering the woods of northern Michigan or wading waist deep in a river searching for trout. Black coffee and a deep love of Hemingway and Huxley fuel the dozens of tales London has penned.

London is the bestselling author of the novella "Pull of the Tide," as well as numerous short stories and articles.

Connect with London on Instagram at @londonthewriter.

Walter John Coburn (October 23, 1889 – May 1971) was born in White Sulphur Springs, Montana Territory, on October 23, 1889. His father, a pioneer cattleman, arrived in Montana Territory in 1863 and founded the Circle C Ranch, one of the largest outfits in the Northwest at the time. Walt gained his cowboy experience which served as material for his future fiction and non-fiction stories as a "$40 a month cowhand" on the Circle C.

From his first accepted story in 1922 until the demise of the pulp western serials in the 1950s, Coburn gained a reputation as "king of the pulp westerns." He published more than 1,000 stories and 40 books. At one point he was producing 600,000 published words a year, and he kept that pace up for two decades. His stories were particularly noted for their authenticity to the frontier and range experience.

Coburn first came to Arizona in 1916 and ranched with his brothers in Globe. He moved to Prescott in 1927, spent 35 years in Tucson and returned to Prescott for the last 10 years of his life. Coburn committed suicide at the age of 82 on 25 May 1971. His autobiography, , was published posthumously in 1974.

Roy Norton (1869 - 1942) was an American newspaperman and author of pulp fiction, including those in the western and science fiction genres. Regular contributor to magazines like *Cosmopolitan, The Popular Magazine,* etc. Sometimes wrote as *Roy E. Norton.*

About the Editors

Frank Theodat is an American short story writer and anthologist whose fiction draws inspiration from the pulp era. He writes speculative fiction and horror on his Substack, *Pulp on the Edge*. He was a co-founder and the first Editor-in-Chief of *Pulp, Pipe, & Poetry Magazine* and now serves as Editor Emeritus, contributing monthly essays to the *Ink & Grit: Masters of Pulp Fiction* series. He currently edits *The Boys Book* series through his company, P3 Media Group LLC, and lives outside Boston, Massachusetts with his wife and son. You can follow his work on his online newsletter *Campfire Canon: History, Commentary & Rediscovery in Boys' Literature & Pulp Fiction.*

Zack Grafman is a husband, father of 3, and assistant pastor living in the Deep South. His early mornings are spent smoking a pipe on his front porch, reading old books, and outlining his next project. He has written many short stories available on Substack and is working on a debut novel.

www.ingramcontent.com/pod-product-compliance
Lightning Source LLC
LaVergne TN
LVHW090611110826
845146LV00001B/339

* 9 7 9 8 2 3 4 0 4 2 2 2 4 *